8/16

SAN JUAN ISLAND LIBRARY DISTRICT

D0040844

DISCARD

omewhere
Among

Somewhere Among

ANNIE DONWERTH-CHIKAMATSU

A CAITLYN DLOUHY BOOK

ATHENEUM BOOKS FOR YOUNG READERS
NEW YORK LONDON TORONTO SYDNEY NEW DELHI

TO MY CHILDREN
AND OUR JAPANESE AND AMERICAN FAMILY

ATHENEUM BOOKS FOR YOUNG READERS
An imprint of Simon & Schuster Children's Publishing Division
1230 Avenue of the Americas, New York, New York 10020
This book is a work of fiction. Any references to historical events, real people, or real places are used fictitiously. Other names, characters, places, and events are products of the author's imagination, and any resemblance to actual events or places or persons, living or dead, is entirely coincidental.
Text copyright © 2016 by Annie Donwerth-Chikamatsu
Jacket illustration copyright © 2016 by Alessandro Gottardo
All rights reserved, including the right of reproduction in whole or in part in any form.
ATHENEUM BOOKS FOR YOUNG READERS is a registered trademark of Simon & Schuster, Inc.
Atheneum logo is a trademark of Simon & Schuster, Inc.
For information about special discounts for bulk purchases, please contact Simon & Schuster Special Sales at 1-866-506-1949 or business@simonandschuster.com.
The Simon & Schuster Speakers Bureau can bring authors to your live event. For more information or to book an event, contact the Simon & Schuster Speakers Bureau at 1-866-248-3049 or visit our website at www.simonspeakers.com.
Book design by Sonia Chaghatzbanian
The text for this book is set in Adobe Caslon Pro.
Manufactured in the United States of America
0316 FFG
First Edition
10 9 8 7 6 5 4 3 2 1
CIP data for this book is available from the Library of Congress.
ISBN 978-1-4814-3786-8
ISBN 978-1-4814-3788-2 (eBook)

JAPAN 2001

JUNE 2001

PREPARING MYSELF

Not enough room
for me to give
Mom space,
I crouch in my corner
fold
clothes for three seasons
into my suitcase
slide
pencil case, supplies box, assignments, notebooks, and textbooks
into my schoolbag
and slip my NASA pen into my pocket.

I do not want to go
to stay with Obaachan, my Japanese grandmother,
but it cannot be helped.

Every August
I pack my summer homework

shorts and swimsuit
to fly to Northern California with Mom

but this year
I am packing
on a school holiday
the longest day of the year
to go to western Tokyo.

I will miss six months of fifth grade at my school
I will miss our holiday by the sea with Papa before California
I will miss a whole month of having Mom's old room to myself.

My friends will miss the cinnamon balls
wrapped in pepper-red plastic
I always bring back
as souvenirs.

JUNE 21, 2001

DEPARTURE

Our bags sit by the door, ready.
On the balcony
I look up into our patch of sky.

Good-bye, View.

At the door,
fighting tears,
I look into our one-room apartment.

Good-bye, Home.

In the elevator
down
floor by floor
we greet people we see every day
but do not know well.

"Foreigner," says a kindergartener,
grabbing his mother's hand
before they enter.
Somewhere someone
who has never seen me before
says something
at least once a day.

Clenching the NASA pen,

I say "I'm Japanese"
to the top of this boy's head.
Mom and Papa say nothing.

The doors open
I bolt past him
running

to the lobby
to friends holding a sign saying
Good-bye, Ema!

The city's afternoon chimes call children back home.
We would all be saying good-bye anyway
for the day.

No one notices I lose the battle with a tear.

THE LONGEST

We wedge the bags
into the trunk,
on Papa's lap in the front seat, and
under my feet in the backseat
next to Mom.

The hired driver turns
in the opposite direction
of the airport
and the sea.

This trip by car could take twice as long as by train,
but two hours
with bus and train connections
would be too much for Mom.

Inching inland in traffic
on stiff white cotton seat covers,
I watch raindrops splatter
Mom vomits into plastic bags
Papa comforts her
each time
they apologize to the driver.

CROSSING TOKYO

Lights sputter on
lamp by lamp
along Rainbow Bridge.

Headlights blink on
car by car
along the highway.

Bulbs flicker on
office by office
shop by shop
street by street.

The driver's eyes,
lit by the dashboard, study me.
A break in traffic
and his eyes are on the road.

We race a ribbon of light
through twinkling towers
with hours to go.

After eleven years,
I should be used to people
trying to figure me out.
I am not.
I usually try not to say anything out loud.

A BRIDGE

Papa would say I am
one foot here
one foot there
between two worlds
—Japan and America—

binational
bicultural
bilingual
biracial.

There, Americans would say
I am half
    half this
    half that.

Here, Japanese would say
hāfu
if they had to say *something*.

Some people here and there say
I am double.

Mom says I "contain multitudes."
Like everyone else.

MULTITUDES

At home
with Mom and Papa

I am
between

two cultures
two languages
two time zones
every day.

Everywhere I go
here or there
I am different.

Everywhere I go
here or there
people think I know
half or double
what I should know.

Not like anyone else
here or there
I sometimes feel alone
on an island
surrounded by multitudes
of people.

Sometimes
I'd rather be on the moon surrounded by multitudes
of stars.

WATCHERS OF THE SKIES

NASA sent Chiaki Mukai,
the first Japanese woman,
into space in 1994.

Grandpa Bob airmailed me the NASA pen.

NASA sent Mamoru Mohri,
the first Japanese astronaut,
into space again last year.
To help map
millions of miles of Earth.

Think beyond borders
reach for the stars
map your own world

Grandpa Bob has always told me

I can make a mark
no matter what

the NASA pen will work if I'm
upside down,
underwater or in space.

Under any pressure.

I carry it wherever I go
I carry it to school
I carry it to visit Obaachan,
especially.

ARRIVAL

We tumble out of the car
in front of Obaachan's wooden gate
she is all business
paying the driver
and
supervising the bags.

Jiichan, my Japanese grandfather,
is all smiles
being supervised
but
leading us through the low gate.

The palm tree Great-Grandfather
planted before he died
greets us in a waving breeze.

At the entry hall
Obaachan is right behind us
directing us each to our slippers.

Toe to heel, I nudge my shoes off,
slip into slippers, and
before I can do it for myself,
Obaachan turns the toes of my shoes to the door.
Papa helps Mom balance.

I step into the wooden puzzle box
of sliding paper doors
opening one room
to another.

I carry my bag
across the wooden entry floor
down the wooden hall
up the stairs to Papa's old room
where we stay at New Year's.
Then, this house is like an icebox.
Now, in the rainy season, it's like a basement
(Mom mentions in English).
Soon, in summer, it will be like a hot-spring bath.

Jiichan slides the paper door
we slide out of slippers
before stepping onto *tatami*.

He has set the beds out for us
like always when we visit
three futons lie on woven grass flooring
side by side by side

just like at home.

NOT AT HOME

Mom is expecting a baby
and needs to rest.

Teaching English at the university
and attending PTA at my school
has made her too "sick and tired."

Grandpa Bob and Nana
cannot leave their jobs
and come to Japan
so
Obaachan will take care of us here
Obaachan will take charge of my schoolwork

Obaachan will take charge of us

like she always does when we visit.

DOWN TO BUSINESS

Six a.m.
Obaachan charges the stairs
scoots out of slippers
plods across the tatami
and slides open the shutters.
Mom sighs and rolls over.

"Late," Obaachan mutters.

Poor Papa,
tired after that long car ride,
is already up and out
on the train to work.
He forgot to reset the alarm.

Cloudy cool creeps
through the window.
No street noise just
neighbors' tongue scraping
                    tooth brushing
                    throat gargling.

Moving a laundry hanger
of Jiichan's underwear and socks
to a bar
outside the window,
Obaachan huffs, "Late."

I stretch,
fold the futon into the closet,
wait for her cue.

Today is a school day.

My first day
at "Obaachan's School,"
enrolled until summer break
at the end of July.

I don't want to be late.

ORDER

Obaachan barges past my elbow,
empties my schoolbag
onto Papa's old school desk.
Shoved into the corner,
it takes up most of the room.

She pushes the bag
into the storage space on
the straight-back chair,
the only chair in the house.
She says it will sit there
waiting to go to school here in September.

I slide my pencil case and supplies box
into the drawer that's mine when I visit.

Obaachan retrieves them, saying,
"Today's schedule, books, pencil case,
downstairs eight thirty,
breakfast at seven."

She stuffs the rest of my textbooks and notebooks
into a cubbyhole,
smashing one side
of the papery lotus pod
that sits next to a cup of pens.

Before she can toss it out the window,
I tell her
it's old
it's Papa's
it's my favorite thing of his.

Papa has drawers filled with
worn erasers,
rusted pencil cases,
small toys,
old postcards,
and faded notebooks of English exercises
where he practiced phrases like "I have a pen"
over and over.

My favorite thing, really, is the room itself.
Papa had his own room.

A ROOM OF HER OWN

But Mom's room
at Grandpa Bob's and Nana's
is even better.

Her teacups
collected from all fifty states
line the shelves Nana built for them
over her desk.

Summer by summer,
tucked in flower-scented sheets
fresh from the dryer,
on a footed bed
in a room just right
(not too cold and not too hot),

I would watch the nightlight twinkle
along the rims of the cups and saucers.

Mom did the very same thing,
watching her collection grow
state by state
summer by summer.

A CORNER

At home
a bookshelf and a chest of drawers
in our shared room is the only room
I have.
I do my homework at the table before dinner.
Our one room is too small
for the desk Obaachan and Jiichan
wanted to buy me when I started first grade.

Obaachan insisted with suggestions.

I have heard Mom say
the first Japanese she learned was
"Mind your business."

She probably said it about the desk,
but I have never heard her say it to Obaachan.

When we visit,
Mom complains under her breath.
Obaachan complains behind closed doors.
Paper doors.

I am glad Mom got her way.
If I had a desk,
there would be no room for this baby
at home.

CORNERED

I will have to share my corner
with this baby.

I always wanted a little sister.
A little brother would be okay.

Any way
sister or brother
I have five months
to wait
for someone like me—

this baby

who will look like me
understand me
and belong with me.

Five months
will be a long time
to stay here.

Five months
will be a long time
to calm Mom.

Five months
will be a long time
to please Obaachan.

I am worried.

WITH GOOD REASON

First day down for breakfast,
textbooks in hand,
I am alone.
Mom still has morning sickness
any time of day.

Late at five past seven,
I ask for a tray for her.
Obaachan says about me
(or Mom?)
"Best to keep a schedule."

Obaachan serves Mom upstairs;
she doesn't trust me with the tray.

I begin to clear dirty dishes from thc table;
Obaachan tells me to prepare for school.

I see it will be difficult to do
my helping-at-home assignment
this summer.

I set out my books, my pencil case, my NASA pen.
Obaachan tells me ink is not allowed.
I'm in fifth grade. I know that!
But I don't say anything.

Jiichan smiles at me
and tells me we're testing
the water.
Somehow he thinks
we will all live together someday.

I don't have the heart to tell him
I already want to go home.

0

And I won't tell Jiichan

I don't want to live
with Obaachan

he knows

I feel closer to him.

I think Jiichan knows

it is hard
to feel close
to Obaachan.

BELONGING WITH

I am never alone in any of these rooms!

I keep school hours
on a cushion
at the table
in front of the TV
where we have meals
where we have tea
where Jiichan sits most of the day.

I miss being on my own
going to school
going to the park
going to the shops
in my neighborhood.

Whenever we go out,
Jiichan carries my *boshi techo*,
the medical-record booklet from the city office
with *Satoh*,
the name we share,
on the cover.

He says, "Just in case."

But I know it's because
we don't look like
we belong together.

My upside-down crescent-moon eyes,
dark brown but not so dark that you can't see the black spokes
that circle my pupils
are just like Papa's
but
my high-bridge nose
chestnut hair
milk-white skin
are just like Mom's.

WHERE AM I FROM?

People ask,

A-me-ri-ka?

That's what it is called here.

Not "United States."
Maybe because the Japanese language
doesn't have some of those sounds.
Like in Mom's name, Maribeth.
Me-ri-be-su.

"It was good pronunciation practice for Papa," she says.

Japanese pronunciation wasn't easy for Mom, either.

She thought she was saying "Great-Grandfather,"
but because of a mistake with one vowel
she was really calling Obaachan's father
"Honorable Old Fart."

BECAUSE OF AN EXTRA CONSONANT

There can be a problem with my name.
Choosing a Japanese name is complicated.
The number of ink strokes
in the *kanji* characters,
the number of syllables,
and the sound
have to be carefully considered.
For good luck. And bad.

Obaachan consulted family registers,
books, and priests.

Grandpa Bob and Nana asked
for a name
they could pronounce.
There are sounds in Japanese
that English doesn't have.

Papa came up with Ema
Obaachan suggested *E-mi-ri*
Emily in English
with the spelling headache of *r* versus *l*.
Mom's university English students drive her crazy with that.

So Papa put his foot down
choosing a name without family consultation.
Ema, *Eh-ma*.

It was not on Obaachan's list of possibilities.

Trying to smooth things, Jiichan said,
"It sounds like the name for shrine plaques."
(He meant the ones for wishes and prayers.)

Mom liked the meaning of the kanji choices,
"mercy" and "truth."

Americans call me *Em-ma*.
They don't know
that extra consonant makes my name
sound like the Japanese name
for God of Hell.

The god who stands at the gate and chooses who should enter.

OF COURSE

No one ever *thinks* of any of that
when they see or hear my name,

Mom says,

it's like thinking of a forest when you hear Mr. Forrest.

Still, I insist on *Ema*
here.

This baby's name will
have good kanji choices
and will be
easy to say
in both languages.

I will make sure of this.

UNNAMED BABY

We don't know
if this baby is a boy or a girl.

Every month Mom has a doctor's appointment.
Every month Mom has a sonogram.
Every month Mom refuses to know.

No name
for a boy or a girl
has been suggested or discussed.

Mom is waiting to see this baby's face.

Other babies have almost come but were lost.
And this baby was almost lost too.

So far, Obaachan is silent about baby names.

This no-name no-face baby has a lot of power.

BUT NOT ENOUGH

To keep Papa here with us

he needs more hours in the day:

working fourteen hours a day
commuting four hours
with
notes from me
beside his midnight dinner rice bowl
notes from him
beside my morning breakfast cereal bowl,
Papa was only sleeping here.

Obaachan convinced him to leave
on our second Sunday here
he packed his bag
to go home
telling me
not to cling
not to cry
not to worry.

I feel stuck on the ground.

I look up into the palm tree
and imagine it
reaching for the sky
reaching up over the houses
reaching outward with
its big leaf hands pulling at Papa
down closer to the bay
up closer to the sky
in our company apartment
paying low rent
saving for a house
saving for this baby and me.

Papa is not home without us
calls every night
speaks to Mom,
this baby,
and me.

It is not enough.

NEITHER HERE NOR THERE

Papa only on the weekend
Grandpa Bob and Nana only on the phone
this summer
I will miss them.

Grandpa Bob smiles
all the time

when I am with him
in America

he sings
“Me and My Shadow.”

I am his shadow.

Nana sings I am her sunshine.

Jiichan knows the song;
one verse of that,
the happy birthday song,
and some basics he learned
from American soldiers in Japan after World War II,
are his only English.

Obaachan only knows the happy birthday song.

All of them sing that to me over the phone.
I never spend my birthday with any of them.

And because school lets out in late July,
I never spend
the Fourth of July, Independence Day,
with Grandpa Bob and Nana.

I never spend
the seventh of July, *Tanabata*, the Star Festival
with Obaachan and Jiichan.
Until this year.

Because of this baby.

JULY 2001

STAR RIVER

Obaachan hands me
a musty children's book about Tanabata.
I hold back a sneeze.

She tells me to read it in my spare time.
I hold back a comment.

I know the story!

The sky god turned his daughter and son-in-law
into stars after she neglected her cloth weaving and
he neglected his cow herding.
He allowed them to meet once
in July.

I hear
or watch
or perform the story

every year
at my school.

One time
I was
the star daughter
separated from my star husband
by the Milky Way
waiting
for July seventh
for clear weather
for magpies to gather
to make a bridge with their wings
so we could meet.

Most times I was a magpie
with paper wings.

STACK OF PAPER

I let Obaachan
show me how
to make a lantern,
          chain, and
          fishnet
to hang on a bamboo branch
for our first Tanabata together.

I don't tell her
I know how
to make lanterns,
          chains, and
          fishnets.

She should know I make them
every year to decorate our class branch.

I do it her way,
mirroring her folds
and cuts.

She eyes my every move.
I cut too deeply
into the fold
of the lantern;
it falls in pieces
from my hands.

She does not have patience
about wasting paper.

I glue the pieces together
into shooting stars.

BAMBOO FOR TANABATA

Obaachan hands Jiichan
one thousand yen
shoos us out of the house
tells us where to go

all the way to the flower shop
I tag behind
like goldfish poop.

Coming back
I am like a caught fish
clutching the tip
of the shop's tallest,
fullest bamboo branch.

Its bobbing leaves

make me twitch, giggle, and sneeze
at least two times,

but I'm glad for the shade.

I sometimes forget,
on purpose,
the old-lady parasol Mom makes me carry.

RETURNING WITH BAMBOO

The pine gate rattles
gara gara
along its runner.

Jiichan bows low

to enter

I bow too
even though
I can make it through
without bending.

I let go
of the branch;
it bounces and whacks
the top of the gate frame.

Jiichan runs water
into a jar

placed at the front door
the branch will not stand
up straight by itself, so
along the garden wall
we comb fern shadows
for rocks.

He smiles,
remembers
hunting colorful eggs
I brought here
in a basket
when I was four.

We feed the mouth of the jar
one,
two,
three rocks
drop from our hands
plop plop
chapon chapon
into the belly of the jar
to help the branch stand
tall.

WISH RULE

When Obaachan sees the size of the branch
she says, "Looks greedy."
She hands me a short stack of narrow paper strips.

She stresses me

telling me not to wish for *things*.

I know that.

"Health and happiness and good fortune," she says.

BUT—

Wishing on paper strips,
birthday candles,
and first stars,
I ask for one thing—
a room of my own.

At home
Papa and Mom and I
eat, sleep, study, work, and watch TV
in the same room.
Only the toilet has a room of its own.

MY WISHES

I choose a sky-blue strip of paper,
use my NASA pen
to write my secret blue-sky wish.

Reaching through leaves
and decorations
I hang my wish at the back
of the bamboo
so no one can read it.

So Obaachan can't read it.

I make a healthy-baby wish too.

I don't write *sister*.
It's too late to wish for that.
It has already been decided
Obaachan reminds me
if ever I say "little sister" out loud.

I put my wish
Healthy Baby
where Obaachan can see it.
And another:
Better Skill in Crafts.

These wishes will surely make her happy.

OBAACHAN'S WISHES

Papa always says his happiness is us
tells me how he and Mom
were bound to be together.

Bound to her by a red thread
tied to their smallest fingers,
he pulled her here
from across the ocean.

"It had been decided," he says.

Obaachan must believe that too
somewhere in her heart
she believes in fate;
she never does anything to cross it.

Don't kill a spider at night!
Don't point with your chopsticks!
Don't wear new shoes on a cloudy day!

But she doesn't know why
Mom mumbles
when she enters the garden gate.

I heard Obaachan say once
behind a closed paper door,

"She grumbles about lowering her head when entering."

Mom doesn't mind the low gate.
No one tells Obaachan
Mom mumbles about passing
under the ladder at the front door
there
for Jiichan
to climb up to water Great-Grandfather's bonsai
on the roof of the porch,
the sunniest spot.

For the health of the bonsai
Papa told me not to tell Obaachan
that some Americans believe passing under a ladder
is bad luck.

Obaachan was the first to hang her wishes.
She is wishing for our health and good fortune.
She forgot our happiness.

JIICHAN'S WISH

I watch each pen stroke
of Jiichan's wish,
the only wish he makes,

for a happy home.

I make that wish too, so
Jiichan has a better chance to get it.

COMPROMISE

Hanging Tanabata wishes
is not Mom's custom.

I make and hang a wish for her

Healthy Baby.

I write it as neatly as I can
in English
so Obaachan will think
Mom made a wish.

So Obaachan has one
less thing to fuss about.

I translate the wish to her.

Two healthy-baby wishes
double the chance
Obaachan will know
we know
what to do
for Tanabata.

PAPA'S WISH

Papa calls
and asks me to write and
hang his wish
on the bamboo.

His wish is the same as Jiichan's wish.

A Happy Home.

Everyone,
even Obaachan, agrees
our job
is to keep Mom calm

for this baby

we need a happy home
here
for at least the summer.

SHARED TRAGEDY

At dinner, after
wish making and wish hanging,
no one says anything
except the TV and Mom.

A newscaster reports on the *Ehime Maru*,
a Japanese fishing ship
struck and sunk
by an American submarine
last February.

Mom reacts to every detail of the accident.

"Such a tragedy."

American divers had to map out
a plan before searching
and trying to raise the wreckage
from the ocean floor.

"Such a big job."

High school students,
teachers,
and crew are dead or missing.

"Such a sad story."

No one says anything
except the TV and Mom.

JULY 1, 2001

NO NEWS VIEWING FOR MOM

The next morning
I ask Mom
to sit at a place setting of dishes
so her back is to the TV.

I want to watch, I tell her.

The problem is she can still hear it.

SUMMER DRESS BATTLE

Upstairs,
Mom pulls back the ties of my cotton dress
close to my body.
Downstairs,
Obaachan loosens them.

Upstairs,
Mom tightens.
Downstairs,
Obaachan loosens.

Upstairs,
pulled tight,
I hear—

Fans!
Altar candles!
The kitchen stove!

Downstairs,
let loose,
I hear—

Stay cool!

Safety versus coolness.

KEEPING PEACE

I agree with Obaachan.
I want to be cool everywhere I go.
But I don't tell Mom.
And I don't understand—

Obaachan should be trying
to help Mom
stay calm.

Tightening and loosening
my dress myself
is impossible.

I don't want to get Jiichan in trouble
so I don't ask for help.

To avoid this battle for Mom
I start wearing shorts.
One pair on.
One pair on the laundry hanger.

Shorts are not cool, but
less ironing *and* less fussing
is best.

A BREEZE FLUTTERS

Wishes at doorways
of neighbors
of shops
of stations
of shrines
of schools

ding ding
chirin chirin

painted glass chimes
tell which way
the breeze blows

ding ding
chirin chirin

withered bamboo leaves
wave good-bye
as it goes

ding ding
chirin chirin

colored paper strips
push wishes
toward the stars.

AS WE COME AND GO

Our wishes remind us
of our hope

to try better
to do better
to be better.

Under the stars

with prayer

our wishes gather power.

Jiichan is praying a lot lately.

UNANNOUNCED

The doorbell gurgles along a wire
and buzzes into the room where we sit.
I have never heard it before.
Deliverymen just open the front door and shout.

From the entry hall, Obaachan calls for me.
Mom's co-teacher, Dorrie,
has Wednesdays off and
has shown up without telephoning.

Obaachan makes sure
I make sure
she puts on guest slippers.

Scuffing down the hall
Dorrie slides out of them
takes them off and
carries them.

Obaachan follows her,
inspecting her sweaty footprints
on the shiny floor
and disappears into the laundry room for a rag.

I tell Dorrie to keep going.

Seeing her holding slippers,
Mom hushes a giggle.

She flushes with excuses
seeing the sparklers Dorrie brought, and
gushes with happiness
seeing the books she unpacks.

BEST MEDICINE

Mom and Dorrie laugh and gossip
and after two cups of cold barley tea
Dorrie goes to the toilet room.
She steps out
onto tatami wearing the toilet slippers.
Obaachan muffles shock and busies herself with rags.

I have been to friends' houses; their mothers are not so picky.

Later, while Mom naps,
Obaachan strongly suggests
we discourage visitors, and
mentions dusty,
                sweaty,
                holey socks
on the floors
where we sit,
                eat,
                and sleep.
Besides, my lessons were disturbed, Obaachan says.

I gently tell Mom.

She is disappointed,
almost a little mad, but says,

"Good thing my supervisor didn't come—
his feet stink."

She tells me stinky-feet stories about
how the faculty avoids
end-of-year parties at restaurants
where you have to take your shoes off.

We have lots of what Mom calls
"belly laughs."

Good for this baby. Good for us.

ON THE OTHER SIDE OF THE WORLD

A day late
but at the same time
fireworks are bursting
in America's air
Mom and I are eating a midmorning
bowl of yogurt
with bottled blueberry sauce
and a Japanese cherry on top

in place of our traditional
evening dessert of
raspberry and blueberry crumble
topped with vanilla ice cream
(no oven at Obaachan's).

America's Independence Day
is not a school holiday
but Obaachan lets me have today
off from studies.

Noon here
night there
a news clip at lunch
is the first time
I've seen fireworks in America
in real time
on *their* fourth of July.

JULY 5, 2001

FEELS LIKE SHOOTING STARS

bursting
sparkling
fizzling

in my heart

I missed
Tanabata
with my friends at school
making decorations
making wishes
and singing songs

without them

for the first time

I feel
how Mom must feel
being far away
from celebrations.

I can only watch
and sing along
with children on TV,

“Bamboo leaves
rustle and sway
at the eaves

Stars twinkle
on gold and silver sand

I have written
on colorful paper strips

Stars twinkle
watching from above.”

JULY 7, 2001

THE DAY AFTER

Obaachan stands over
Jiichan untying paper
            stripping leaves
            feeding flames
in a rusted paint can

to send our wishes
up, up, up
into the universe.

They will come back to us
if our hearts are pure.

From Papa's window
I watch

ashes
curl and climb
up, up, up
into the air.

Great-Grandfather's palm
bats
and catches
wisps.

Obaachan climbs the ladder
fans a newspaper
with one hand
to free them
up, up, up
away from the tree.

Burning trash is forbidden,
but Obaachan risks paying a fine.

I hear her tell Jiichan
no one gets a ticket for burning wishes.

RETURNED

Obaachan's slippers
clobber
the stairs

up, up, up
to Papa's room.

She knocks
don don don don don

finds my wrist
presses
my blue-sky wish
into my hand
and says,

"An only child can have a room alone."

HEATING UP

MY SELFISHNESS

Obaachan says nothing else to me.
But I know—
"Thinking about wrong behavior
is punishment."

Everyone in this house
has no brothers or sisters.

Everyone in this house
knows I want a brother or sister.

Everyone in this house
wants this baby.

I don't tell Mom about the wish.

She would tell me
we make our own luck
with our thoughts.
Besides,
a school friend, Hiroko,
has a little sister
and a room of her own.
So, it's not out-of-this-world
impossible.

And if wishes do have power,
the *Healthy Baby* wish

I made for myself and for Mom
is double strong
and will cancel
my room wish,
but

just in case

for this baby's sake

I put my blue-sky wish
in a safe place.

FOLLOWING OBAACHAN'S RULES

Along with my school assignments

starting today

Obaachan makes me read from
a copy of
Customs and Manners
she pulled from Papa's closet.

She stands over me
neglecting dirty dishes
in the kitchen.

My NASA pen
with the blue-sky wish
rolled
around its ink cartridge
sits beside my eraser,
three pencils, and a sharpener.

Obaachan reminds me
again today like every day
not to use ink for schoolwork.

OUR SPACE AND TIME

This baby hears
more Japanese here—
Obaachan's fussing
about Jiichan
leaving tea rings on the table,
bruising tomatoes on shop errands,
forgetting something on her list

the TV blaring
recipes,
drama,
and news
all day long.

Before I was born,
Mom read English books to me.
That's why my English is so good, she says.

Upstairs,
between meals,
Mom lies or sits on her futon
reading magazines and books
to this baby.

The fan's propeller head
clicks back and forth
pushing water-thick air toward them.

Upstairs,
after school hours,
we speak English together
to this baby
or
we listen to music
or
she reads to us
while I sit
at her futon
fanning a magazine or
at the desk
rattling Papa's dried lotus pod.

When the city chimes call children home
from the park or friends' houses,
I start homework exercises before dinner.

On the phone I tell Papa, "I think it's getting too hot for this baby."

BEYOND THEIR CONTROL

Papa has arranged
installation of

air-conditioning
in Great-Grandfather's old room
for Mom
and
cable TV in the family room
for Jiichan.

Obaachan, standing over the servicemen,
mumbles, "We don't need this."

I agree we don't need
more channels of TV.

STAYING COOL

Mom will endure
the heat without AC
as long as possible

she says

that she'd rather have
a big telephone bill than a big electricity bill

that she doesn't like to
come in and out of a cool room, but I know

she really doesn't want to
be downstairs.

When Mom's friends call
Obaachan makes Jiichan pull the telephone and fan
from the TV room
into Great-Grandfather's room
after Mom comes downstairs
so she doesn't trip over the cords.
(No danger of her falling down the stairs—
if she takes a deep breath, she'll get stuck in the stairwell.)

Mom sits on a cushion
calm as Buddha
telling her friends

she can endure non-stop TV
                              no Internet access
                              no sweets
anything
for this baby.

HOT SEAT

Meanwhile,
there is no fan for us.

I fold a piece of newspaper into one.

Jiichan opens the closet,
finds a collection of
big, stiff paper fans,
advertisements from shops.

He gives me a choice.

I choose one and swat the air
SWOOSH.

It's not easy to hold a pencil
and a fan at the same time

so Jiichan fans me
while I work math problems.

Shaped like a dish
of blue shaved ice
the fan looks *cool.*

But it's not.

WHITE PAPER, "THE DEFENSE OF JAPAN 2001"

I am trying to concentrate on
a list of kanji
filling in
box after box
stroke by stroke
page after page, but

Jiichan turns up the TV volume.
He does not miss the news
ever since North Korea shot missiles into Tokyo Bay
a few years ago.

Today,
lots of discussion
criticism
and protests
from Korea and China especially

about recent Japanese textbooks.

They say Japan should write more about
and apologize more for
World War II.

I have multitudes to learn.

When Papa calls
I tell him,
“Mom needs earplugs.”

JULY 12, 2001

HOT WATER

Bath time comes early.

Mom has always been first in line at Obaachan's.

Papa told them Americans don't soak in the same water
but, at home, we fill the bathtub only once too,
and I am first in line.

Obaachan insists Mom go first. Then me.
Especially because of this baby.

Obaachan gets her way.

Mom comes out peach pink
complaining

the water is too warm again.

I've heard Obaachan fussing
at Jiichan
saying a cool bath will shock the baby.

Obaachan gets her way.

Mom tells Papa
Obaachan is trying to kill us.

Papa tells Mom to cool off
to stay calm
to choose her battles
reminding her
he will be here on Sunday.

I take the phone to Obaachan.

"You shouldn't come," she tells Papa. "Save energy."

Obaachan gets her way

until Papa shows up the next day
on a thunderous Friday the thirteenth.

AT GREAT EXPENSE

After much money
many hours
and much energy

Papa arrives

bringing Mom a portable music player with headphones,
telling her to wear them especially at meals, and

convincing her to move downstairs into AC
at least on humidity mode.

He moves our futons, books, and clothes downstairs

instructs her and everyone on how to use the AC

reminds her and Obaachan both (separately)

to stay cool (calm)

—at all costs—

for this baby.

PURSE STRINGS

Obaachan holds the money in the household.

She plans
money for daily expenses,
payment for bills,
and an allowance for Jiichan.

The rest is saved.

Mom says Obaachan is sitting
on a mountain of money

saved from
scrimping on Jiichan's salary
living rent-free with Great-Grandfather
inheriting everything as his only child.
Jiichan's retirement pension tops the pile each month.

A bell hangs from the zipper pull of Obaachan's money
purse;
the deeper she digs, the more it jingles
its warning:
Too much. Too much. Too much.

Mom and Papa share money matters;
Mom works outside the house like Nana.

Here in this house, we are guests.
Obaachan won't take money.
Our hands are tied.

We are marionettes dangling from Obaachan's tight fists.

Papa is trying to loosen her grip
on everything.

He has a hard time leaving money
with Obaachan for expenses;
she argues with him.
He has a hard time leaving Mom and me;
we cling to him.

He heads back, tired,
uncomplaining
in rain and thunder for work on Saturday.

LOTUS WATER

Rainy Saturday morning of cartoons
Great-Grandfather and Great-Grandmother smile at me
(without showing teeth)
from faded photos
on the family altar next to the TV.

They have pleasant smiles every day
while I do my schoolwork
while we eat
while we watch TV.
Today,
I ask Jiichan if I ever met them.
Great-Grandmother, no,
but he tells me a story of
a four-year-old me
making Great-Grandfather smile by

dipping his cane
down to the muddy bottom
of a blue
wide-mouthed
potbellied jar
of rising lotuses,

making prints
of the wet cane tip
on the stone path,

watching them evaporate,
then searching for them.

The cane is gone
cremated with him
and his favorite hat
and wool winter coat.

The lotus was burned in the garden when it died.

Shards of its jar are
at the bottom of potted plants.

Jiichan says we use Great-Grandmother's dishes every day.

LEFT BEHIND

Great-Grandfather's calligraphy inkwell is mine.
Made of stone,
it couldn't go with him.

I keep it in Papa's desk.

Bonsai trees, metal garden tools,
et cetera,
were left behind in the garden.
Jiichan waters, clips, and
sifts through Great-Grandfather's
et cetera
left untouched for years
until now.

Clearing out things too early?
What would neighbors think?

Obaachan says

considering the right way to act
is a sign of respect.

Today she mentions again
the old sink rusting near the garden wall.
Non-burnable
and too big for trash day,

it will have to be
hauled away.

She doesn't want to spend the money.

"We're paying for war mentality," Obaachan says.

"Metal was saved
in World War II
to make weapons," Jiichan explains.

EAT WELL WHEN YOU CAN

Obaachan is generous with food.
Cooking is her affection,
passing rice bowls from her hand to ours.

Eat to keep up strength.
She insists I need more than a bowl of cereal at breakfast.
This could be the last meal for a while.
She lived through the bombing of Tokyo in World War II.
Don't leave one grain of rice in your bowl!

She cooks a lot in the morning.
Whatever is left from breakfast
she covers with paper.
That is lunch.
Whatever is left at lunch is part of dinner.

Mom is eating everything
Obaachan cooks at breakfast.

Obaachan is a little pleased, I know,
but today at lunch
before Mom sits down
before she puts headphones on
before she picks chopsticks up
Obaachan instructs her,
"Have small, grow big,"

which means have a small baby to fatten up
which means Mom is eating too much
which means Obaachan is not following
Papa's—at all costs—rule
of keeping Mom calm.

Mom doesn't need more suggestions.

I think she is finishing everything
to avoid
food set out
all day in the heat.
And because she vomits a lot.

I notice Jiichan isn't eating much.

TOO BUSY

Shuttered up in this house
at night
I hear it creak.

I hear Jiichan up late
at night
he does not sleep.

By five thirty a.m.,
except when it is raining,
he's up to sweep
the stone path and the garden.
Sweeping dirt.

Walking to the shops with Obaachan,
I once pointed out a house with a patch of grass

just to show her.

"More work, more water," she said.

WATERING

At commercial breaks
Jiichan moves potted plants,
following a patch of sun
across the garden.

Then at sunset
I watch him
water them
with a tin cup
tied to the end of a bamboo pole,
dipping it
again and again and again
into a pail of water

thump thump
kotsun kotsun
tin against plastic

dribbling it
so the soil doesn't wash away from the roots.

He climbs
to water the bonsai

bump bump slosh slosh
gotsun gotsun *bicha bicha*
the pail against the metal ladder.

In America, Grandpa Bob has a hose.
He stands in one place
and sprays
or puts a sprinkler at the end of it
and goes inside to watch TV.
I took a picture of the sprinkler once and showed it to Jiichan.

He said, "American ingenuity."

"I will bring you a hose someday as a souvenir.
To finish watering faster."

Obaachan said, "The water bill will be big."

MOM SAVES OBAACHAN MONEY

Mom has always complained about
Jiichan's after-dinner cigarette.
Papa told him doctors say,
"Don't smoke around a pregnant woman."

All smells bother Mom now. Even good ones.
Like Jiichan's hair gel.

Today she stops eating her lunch and gags
when Jiichan stirs up his *natto*.
Fermented soybeans are stinky!

So,
Jiichan cannot smoke.
Jiichan cannot wear his hair gel.
Jiichan cannot eat natto.

I know Obaachan doesn't like food limitations
but is happy
about the cigarette warning.

She wants Jiichan to stop smoking.

"Our pension is going up in smoke," she says.

Poor Jiichan.

He has to quit smoking, and
quit eating his favorite food,

and he has messy hair.

NEIGHBORHOOD EYES

Smells know no boundaries.

On this sunny Tuesday
the smell of curry rice, my favorite,
drifts into the garden
midafternoon
from Mrs. Yamada's.
I haven't had curry rice all summer.

Outside the gate,
I linger
near her kitchen window

listening to

ton ton ton

potato, carrot, onion, green pepper, chicken
under the knife on the cutting board

and breathing in

each spicy snap, snap, snap
of packaged broth cubes.

Obaachan, in her kitchen apron,
standing in the entry hall,

tells me when I return,

"Eyes and ears everywhere."

I know the neighborhood
watches manners
and looks out for kids,
but she wants me to know
she saw me lingering.

She is watching me
outside the house too.

Upstairs, at Papa's window,
I enjoy whiffs of
Mrs. Yamada's bubbling curry.

Mom vomits into one of the plastic bags
she tucks at the edge of her futon.

NEIGHBORHOOD EARS

Here, houses huddle
shoulder to shoulder
in groups of five.

Windows peer at one another,
wide open except in winter.
Thin walls, no insulation
let cold in.
Noise comes in and out.

A phone ringing? Could be anyone's.
You can keep score
on sports games without watching.
Tonight Mr. Ito is singing along
to *enka* (not my favorite.)
He is pretty good, though.

You're not supposed to listen
to other people's private matters
to other people talking
to other people watching
but it's hard not to

hear
Mr. Ishii scraping his tongue at six thirty a.m.
Mr. Yamada anytime after six forty-five but before seven.
Jiichan, the first, at five.

Tongue scraping,
throat gargling,
pan shuffling
start the day.

Gargling happens anytime someone returns home:
mothers from errands
children from school and play
salarymen from work late at night.

Hiro Ishii returns after high school cram school
around six p.m.,
our dinnertime.

Mom vomits anytime all day long.
I heard Obaachan apologize to Mrs. Ishii.

SOUND OF SUMMER

At noon,
voices
try to coax me out into the garden
to look for them.

This cycle of cicadas has waited
seventeen years
to crawl up from deep
underground
to shed their outer shells
to sing.

I have enjoyed
cycles of cicada chorus
and cicada hunts
with friends at home.

It's not fair
this sound of summer
starts before summer break.

I stop to listen

to summer

between exercises.

NOTHING WILL CHANGE

Daily summer assignments

extra from Obaachan
and

no one
to play with

no one
to meet

no one
to make friends with

I am

too far away
from the park
from the river
from the shops

stuck at Obaachan's
until school starts September first.

A VISITOR FOR ME

At four p.m.,
the gate rattles;
its rusted red metal bell dings.
High heels click across the stone path.

A teacher from the neighborhood school
presents herself
dressed in a navy blue suit
she impresses Obaachan

even more
for slipping white cotton socks
over her stockings
before sliding into guest slippers.

Obaachan serves glasses of *mugicha*.
The teacher nods toward the glass of cold barley tea
and says, "Thank you."
TV is silent.
Jiichan and Mom too.
We listen to explanations
point by point of

worksheets for practicing skills
schedules for doing summer assignments
schedules for taking supplies the first week
of the fall term in September.

This school and my school
are on the same page.
But
this teacher compliments my Japanese
like I have not spent almost five years in Japanese school
like I have not made good grades in Japanese school
like I am not Japanese.

I do not want to go to her school.

I tell Papa on the phone.
He tells me "*ganbatte*."

I will have to endure
until the semester finishes in December.

I tell him

I will make an effort
to cooperate
to endure with strength and patience

like he told me.

SEA DAY

A national holiday
a break from schoolwork

cicadas are in full song
high in the treetops.

I watch Jiichan digging
through the shed
for Papa's old net.

He stops
takes off his hat, and
wipes his head.
He looks tired.

"I am too old for cicada catching," I tell him.

We take a break for

cicada listening
on the stoop outside the TV room
until mosquitoes chase us inside.

Jiichan offers to walk down to the river.

"I am too tired," I tell him.

He smiles
gratitude.

JULY 20, 2001

CALL OF THE SEA

Papa cannot afford to come to Obaachan's.

He calls to tell me to look
in the bottom desk drawer.
It's like digging through
a treasure chest of his past.

What am I looking for?

My hand knows before I do

something feels different
from all the metal and plastic—

a small chipped shell

I hold
to my ear

hold my breath

and hear

the sea.

I rush downstairs
to hold it to Mom's belly

for this baby to hear
then to Mom's ear.
I let Jiichan hear.
(Obaachan is too busy with dinner.)

Thank you, Papa,
for this Sea Day holiday.

JULY 20, 2001

LOW AND HIGH

Eyes lowered,
not watching the TV,
Jiichan and Obaachan
chew in small circles
and swallow
grilled fish, rice, and summer tomatoes,
listening to

an update of the *Ehime Maru*,
its mast will be dynamited
girded
and lifted
from the sea.

I look across the table at Mom
her back to the TV screen;
the beat of her favorite Train tune
bangs in her headphones,
blasting a smile on her face.

She pinches
the fish on her plate
folds back
its scales
and lifts the spine
from its flesh.

Using chopsticks was the first table manners she learned here.

Patting her hand and pointing
to the news coverage of
the anniversary of Apollo 11,
America's moonwalk,
I bring her back to Earth.

Mom smiles at me.
She and Grandpa Bob and Nana share this memory.
Jiichan and Obaachan and Papa watched here at this table.
Now Mom and Jiichan and Obaachan and I share this,
saying, "Wow,"
with each detail,
each image.

JULY 21, 2001

LETTING OUT

Bringing in the laundry
will be my summer
helping-at-home
homework.
Starting before it counts,
I lean outside Papa's window
snapping
socks
underwear
pajamas
towels
rags
from hangers,

watching

students pass by
toting home
each day
a different bag

paint sets
sewing kits
calligraphy sets
gym clothes
desk supply boxes.

I know it's the last day of school
when I see the bags of
indoor shoes
and padded emergency hoods
we keep on the backs of our school chairs
for fire and earthquake drills.

I try not to tell Mom how much
I do not want to go to school here.

BLUE STARBURSTS

Mothers haul home
from school
potted morning glories
in their bicycle baskets.

Part of first graders'
summer homework is to:
            keep their morning glory alive
            watch it grow
            take notes
            collect seeds
            make a paper gift box
to present to new first graders
when the new school year starts next April.

Morning glory care builds a connection between students
for the future.

Next year in sixth grade
we will grow pots of rice
at my old school
and pass along the seeds to the fifth graders.

I am not a part of this neighborhood.

WITH A LITTLE HELP FROM MY FRIENDS

I am not going to think about
September
when I will start school
here

in a class
where everyone has been together
since the first day of school in April

where everyone has a group of friends
since the first day of first grade

where everyone has a place in the neighborhood
since they were born.

I will be the outsider.

But I'm not going
to think about that now.

I've already written but not sent
summer greeting cards
(from Papa's leftovers)

to my friends
in my old neighborhood
telling them to watch for me

with my papa this year
at the summer festival.

This will be my free time for fun.

I'm going to think about that.

THOUGHTS OF FUN

Wearing *yukata*
going back with Papa
to enjoy
eating octopus legs on sticks, cotton candy in bags
snagging water balloons, plastic prizes
scooping goldfish, super balls
watching fireworks, looking for friends
firing rockets, sparking sparklers
these things I am thinking, asking
but
Obaachan reminds me
how hard the trip is for Papa

tells me not to ask to go
tells me Papa needs to save energy
tells me there will be fireworks here in August.

Obaachan gets her way.

Jiichan mails my corrected,
ink-smudged greeting cards.

I'm too embarrassed
to send them
too embarrassed

to hand them
to the postwoman.

I can watch my hometown fireworks on TV.
It won't be the same.

Obaachan is a fun killer.

FREE TIME?

Mom suggests things to do
to keep me busy.

How about reading English aloud?
She brought plenty of storybooks.

"That's boring," I tell her. (Actually, it's too hard.)

Needlepoint?
She brought her bag of work.

"That's complicated." (Actually, it's too hot.)

Collage?
She brought scissors.

I have my school scissors and glue bottle.

She selects the magazines
and we begin.

THE PROJECT

I am making a card for American Grandparents Day,
to get it in the mail early
way before September ninth.

Nana likes flower gardening.
Grandpa Bob likes space travel.
Both like rainbow viewing.

I decide to tear not cut
small pieces of paper.
Mom says,
"Oh, like *chigiri-e.*"

I say, "Yes, East meets West,"
something she says when she cooks.

Dabbing the pieces with glue
I fill in my drawings of
flowers falling
from the space shuttle flying
over a rainbow map of America,
something for both Nana and Grandpa Bob.

I tell Mom she can have all the magazine flower photos.

I fill in blank spaces
with my old set of Pocket Monsters crayons

I keep in Papa's desk.

Mom cuts and spells out words

nouns:
peace
future
hope

adjectives:
quiet
strong
harmonious

verbs:
wait . . .

is shc making this an English lesson?

ADDING TO THE LIST

Mom cuts out pictures

filling in a black marker circle
on newspaper
calling it a mandala
saying, “East meets West.”

We laugh.

I find the word “happy,”
cut it out, and give it to her.

She smiles.

I write “Happy Days” in NASA pen ink
at the top of my card.

Japan has Respect for the Aged Day
on September fifteenth this year.
Obaachan says that is not the same thing
as Grandparents Day.

It is a different day.

KILLING FUN

Obaachan makes a schedule of my summer days.

She doesn't give me a break.

A DAY OUT

Jiichan says I need
to get out of the house
to stand in line
to see Miyazaki's newest movie.

TV says it is already his biggest hit.

Obaachan suggests
going on Tuesday,
seniors' free admission day
at the cinema two stations away.

IN THE ENTRY HALL ON TUESDAY

Doors of the shoe cabinet slide
back and forth;
Jiichan is selecting his shoes.
Obaachan mumbles
low, deep.

Mumble, slide. Mumble, slide. Mumble, slide.

Jiichan stands in silence.

Obaachan is having a conversation
with the shoe cabinet.

I step past them
into my shoes
and out the door.

Gacha!
snaps
the cabinet
where Jiichan's best shoes are stored.

A few comments about whether
he needs his best shoes or not
and
the conversation ends.

Obaachan makes suggestions to me
and Mom before we go out

about handkerchiefs,
about socks (holes!)
about shoes
about umbrellas
about . . .

Poor Jiichan.
He took her attention away from me today.

ON THE WAY TO THE TRAIN STATION

My parasol shades
the back of Jiichan's heels.
A pair of swallows
spiral and duck
one at a time
under the awning of a soba shop.

"Lucky place," Jiichan says, "to have swallows choose you."

We pass
the clump of trees,
a performance hall of cicadas,
where a group of gravestones sit.
Cool air invites us in.

But you should never go into a graveyard
unless
you have connections to a grave

Obaachan has always warned me

not to go inside for cicadas

not to even look inside.
But I look.

I am bound
to look
from the corners of my eyes

to say sorry
to the old stones

broken stones
no one takes care of
no one visits
no one sees

except
my eyes
my eyes are drawn there.

Looking
back at me
today,
a boy's cold eyes
make me look away.

My foot kicks a pebble.
It bounces off Jiichan's butt.
I say, "Sorry."
He doesn't notice.

AT THE TRAIN STATION

On our own
with Jiichan's pocket money,
we buy two train tickets,
two salmon-filled *onigiri,*
and two cans of cold tea.

He hands one of each to me.

I place the can on my neck and sigh.
Jiichan laughs.

On the platform
we find a bench
in the shadow of Mitsubishi Bank
at the south exit.

My first bite
crackles seaweed
and
flakes down my dress.
His first swig
dribbles tea
and
streams down his chin.

He doesn't wipe it away.
On my last bite of rice, salmon, and seaweed

he hands me his handkerchief

knowing I always forget mine.

Even if Obaachan reminds me,
I avoid taking off my shoes
and running upstairs
by telling her,
"Somebody's always handing out tissues at the station."

Today no tissues.

Sweat beads on Jiichan's cheek.
We sigh together.
And wait.

AT THE CINEMA BOX OFFICE

An hour
or two in line
we wait
just to get to the ticket window.

The clerk hesitates.

Jiichan reaches through the glass
to show the cover of my *boshi techo*
to show my birth date
to show I can get the elementary school student rate.

I am big for my age, but no one mentions it
here
now.

Someday I will have my own photo ID

when I am in junior high
no one will ask me my age.

Jiichan doesn't have to show
his ID for free senior admission.
He looks his age.

IN THE LOBBY

A poster for *Pearl Harbor*
stands out
by itself.

Not many people stand in line
for that movie.

AFTER THE MOVIE

Jiichan says he's worried about nightmares.

—I am thinking of baby names—

Yubaba, the old witch in the movie,
changes the names of her workers
so they forget who they are

so she has power over them.

I am thinking this baby needs a name now.

I tell Jiichan, "Don't worry. I never have nightmares,"
even though
being spirited away
forgetting my name
and
Yubaba herself
scare me.

I look for the graveyard eyes.
They aren't there on the way back.

Later I realize

maybe Jiichan is worried he will have nightmares.

AUGUST 2001

HIROSHIMA ANNIVERSARY

Every house is burning
incense
except this one
because of Mom.

TVs blare the same scene—
crushes of people
at the broken dome
at the Tower of a Thousand Cranes
at ground zero where America dropped an atomic bomb.

A bell strikes the time
Obaachan and Jiichan bow their heads
sirens there blast
sirens here cry
echo
slip away

a moment of silence

cicadas
screech
sizzle
wail

wind chimes
strike house by house
incense
reaches my nose

doves scatter
toward the sky of Hiroshima
TV by TV
like the neighborhood is taking flight.

Behind closed doors,
Mom is vomiting into one of her plastic bags.

AUGUST 6, 2001

ANNIVERSARY OF AMERICA DROPPING ANOTHER ATOMIC BOMB ON JAPAN

Obaachan and Jiichan each light
one stick of incense
snuff them out
after praying at the family altar.

pin pon pan pon
the jingle
for public announcements
and emergencies
alerts us
to
a moment of silence
beginning at
11:02 a.m.

Channels switch to
the mayor of Nagasaki speaking out
against nuclear weapons,
warning about them
expanding into space.

His voice echoes
house to house.

Sirens tell us to be silent.
We bow.

A loudspeaker there and here tells us,
“Finished.”

Mom is with us.
Jiichan is lost to us.

He disappears behind his eyes,
a boy again
in the hills
watching
outside Nagasaki.

I have never seen him like this.
We are usually in America
this time of year.

AUGUST 9, 2001

VISIT TO OBAACHAN'S FAMILY GRAVE

Before leaving the garden,
Obaachan places a small plate of salt
outside the gate
to use when we return.

With tools and a stool,
parasols and incense,
chrysanthemums and canned tea,
Jiichan, Obaachan, and I set out on foot.

We pass
the clump of trees
of broken gravestones
and cicadas.

In the deep cool
a boy with a net
moves into scattered light.
I see his face, his cold eye.
I recognize that look and look away.

I hush a gasp so Obaachan won't know I was looking.

THE VISIT

Dead-of-summer
humid

nothing is hotter than standing on stone,
surrounded by stone.

Shrubs and ornamental trees cast short shade.

Obaachan wanted to come today
on Great-Grandmother's birthday.

She sets up
on the folding stool
under her parasol
like an eel in the shadows
zapping Jiichan
zapping me
with orders:

"Clip this, clip that
Scrub here, scrub there"

with proper tools
in a proper bag
reserved especially
for the graveyard.

TAKING CARE

We
snip snip *choki choki*
stainless steel clippers
rounding
scraggly heads of cedar.

We
shoosh shoosh *goshi goshi*
reed bristles
brushing
hollow names of ancestors.

We
thump thump *kotsun kotsun*
tin cups
watering
wilted plants, crusted stones.

Jiichan and I are lost in robotics.

I am thinking

about the bones
the pieces of bones
in the ceramic jars
under the cover stone
while I am

snipping and shooshing and thumping
arranging flowers and canned tea
lighting incense
praying

for them all.

These are the things we do for the dead.

This is the grave of Obaachan's ancestors.
My ancestors.

There is nothing
no *thing*
left of Jiichan's family
to snip, shoosh, and thump over
in Nagasaki.

NAMES

Jiichan struggles with the incense
trying to put it out before we leave.
A breeze does not help him.

The wooden slats of Buddhist names
given after death
click click against the railing
behind the pillar stone
of Obaachan's family name.

I run my fingers
across relatives' first names
chiseled into the stone
next to the pillar.

Obaachan must think I am checking my cleaning skills.

I am looking at names
looking for possible choices
possible kanji choices
for this baby.

Some I cannot read.
Some I do not like.
None I would choose for this baby.

RETURNING

At the gate
Obaachan pinches and throws
salt at Jiichan's chest

he turns

at his back
she throws another pinch.

He sprinkles salt on her
front and back

then me
front and back
so uninvited spirits
won't follow us through the gate.

ENTERING

A fly enters the front door ahead of us.

A melon has been sitting at the family altar
until it is ready to eat.

It is ready to eat.

The fly is ready.

Mom is there,
round as a melon,
waiting,
ready to eat too.

PHONE JUGGLING

Grandpa Bob tells me he misses my summer visit.
Nana gets on the phone,
says they will visit
after the baby comes,
says she can't wait to get all my sugar.

Grandpa Bob, back on the phone,
asks me how everybody is doing, and
asks if I saw the launch of *Discovery*
(no?)
and describes the fireball thrusting;
its vapor trail
towering
splitting
the clear blue sky.

He tells me two Russians and one American
will dock at the International Space Station.

"We had a joint mission in space twenty-six years ago,"
he tells me. "Back during the Cold War."

We were enemies then.

Before he hangs up, he says, "Give everyone my best."

AUGUST 11, 2001

UP IN ARMS

Jiichan stops mid-crunch
listens, with a mouthful
of rice crackers, to
the TV report of
Prime Minister Koizumi's visit to
Yasukuni Shrine
to pay his respects to the war dead
of World War II.

Some of the war dead
are war criminals
so
other countries express opinions
saying a government official
should not visit the shrine.

China,
North and South Korea, and
America are mad.

Some people here are mad too.

Jiichan swallows
gets up from the table
to pray earlier than usual.

AUGUST 13, 2001

DESERTED

I watch neighbors
leaving for Obon,
rushing for trains
returning to their hometowns
to visit family members
dead or alive.

There are no living relatives visiting
at Obaachan's
except Mom and me
and Papa!
He makes Obaachan bearable.

We dust and wipe
sweep and vacuum
until

pika pika
a sparkling house
and
kuru kuru
a spinning paper lantern
flash and guide spirits of our family
back to visit.

I wonder if any spirits from America will be coming.

PAPA

Came, slept, left.

VICTORY OVER JAPAN DAY

Jiichan surfs through channels
stops at
CNN reporting
the anniversary of the announcement
of Japan's surrender to the United States in WWII,
showing old photos
of crowds
of New York's Times Square
of a famous kiss.

Jiichan listens to the translation.

Mom passes through from the toilet, says,
"Ah! That's a famous photo!"

Mom is rosy-faced.

It *is* a happy picture.

Jiichan has never seen it before.

He says he remembers that day, though.

Mom's face grows redder.

AUGUST 15, 2001

A FIRST

chirin chirin!

From the window, I see
Jiichan standing beside a bicycle,
a small one
for me!

From inside, I hear Obaachan say,
"A used bicycle! You bring other people's luck here!"

Jiichan talks back,
says, "No money for a new bike."

I circle back to the kitchen
before running outside.

A shower of salt
rains from my hand
and pelts the bike.

It is an auspicious day:

I make my own luck
I have a bike here

I make Obaachan laugh.

I think it was a laugh.

ERRANDS

My world becomes a whole lot wider.
Having a bike at Obaachan's house is a wish
I never thought of making.

Jiichan can ride his bike when we go out together.

He says I am a natural,
like a fish in water.
He has forgotten
I ride one at home.

I follow right behind his bicycle
and carry groceries in my basket.
So much easier to shop by bike.

Try carrying bags while balancing a parasol!

The parasol has to stay
in the entry hall.
A city umbrella law says
no umbrellas while riding bikes.

Only problem now—
stopping
and backtracking to pick up
the huge sun hat Mom makes me wear.

AT THE POST OFFICE WITH JIICHAN

Stamp possibilities plaster the bulletin board.

Nana and Grandpa Bob like pretty stamps.
They send packages
with rows of them.

I hand the Grandparents Day card to the postwoman.

A little overweight
two hundred yen,
the price of two canned teas.

I choose four stamps from
the *Seasonal Splendors in Tokyo II* series of
seasonal flowers:
hydrangeas, chrysanthemums, camellias, cherry blossoms
at fifty yen each.

I sponge them onto the card.

The corner of the envelope
is soggy.
The postwoman inspects it
mumbles, hesitates,
but accepts it.

"By September ninth?"

“Before.”

I believe her.
From here to there,
Japan to America,
mail usually goes faster.

Honest.

BY HAND

I'd rather be on a plane
on my way to deliver it.

Summer greeting cards
from my friends
come
one by one
reminding me
I am not forgotten

reminding me
someone somewhere
is having a good summer.

That's usually me,
too.

At Grandpa Bob and Nana's.

NEWS FROM UWAJIMA

Southwest of Tokyo
US Navy officials have come
face to face
to explain plans to bring
nine boys and men
of the *Ehime Maru*
up from under the sea.

They think these sons,
brothers,
fathers,
husbands
are entombed
in the wreck.

I feel the depth
of sadness
in the room

on the officials' faces

on the family members' faces

on Jiichan's face.

I cannot control
a tear from streaking
my face.

I smudge it into my wrist
and join Mom and this baby
in Great-Grandfather's room
cocooned among pillows,
books, and family magazines.

AUGUST 19, 2001

GIANT FISH HEADING TOWARD TOKYO

The TV tracks Typhoon Pabuk,
named after a big fish in Laotian,
raging across Japan,
killing twenty people already,
delaying trains and airplanes.

Papa is stuck at the office
and cannot walk to the train station
to go home.

And a rocket
we've been waiting to watch
is waiting for an airplane
to bring a replacement valve
so it can take off on the twenty-ninth.

AUGUST 21, 2001

CAUGHT

Far inland
we are

bashed by
wind and rain.

Obaachan fusses at Jiichan for not
replacing batteries
in the emergency-supplies shed.

Giant Fish Typhoon catches us
with a dead flashlight

but luckily we don't lose power.

CLEAR SKIES

After four days of rain
of staying inside
Jiichan and I go out.

He is stiff from sitting
but manages raking and sweeping.
Obaachan washes lunch dishes.
Mom naps.

I ride my bike to the shops
to buy sliced pork,
        tomatoes,
        lettuce,
        greens
for dinner
and batteries
for the flashlight.

A mom passes me

a wilted morning glory
in her basket
flutters its way back to school.

Kids my age
kids who may be in class
with me in a week
fill the streets.

Some carry insect nets
some carry cram-schoolbags
some carry groceries in their bicycle baskets.

Kids own the streets today!

No one notices me
no one knows me
and
summer is almost over!

The city chimes tell us to head back
home.

I wish I could.

NEWS BREAK

For my summer read-aloud assignments,
Obaachan makes me stand.
But tonight, after dinner,
I read the assignment,
a happy story
about forest animals,
to Mom's belly.

Jiichan claps when I finish.
Obaachan gives me a low mark for posture
on my performance card.

I tell Jiichan this baby is already learning.

This baby can hear everything we say and do.

Jiichan picks up the newspaper and reads aloud
in Mom's direction.
I suggest the entertainment page.

Jiichan's voice booms like a drum
and makes this baby tap, tap, tap.

That makes Jiichan smile, smile, smile.

He doesn't notice he's missed the evening news.

ON SCHEDULE

The sun comes in and out
every other day.
I finish my summer homework
with multiple repetitions.

Obaachan huffs in relief.

The replacement valve
for
Japan's National Space Development Agency's H2A rocket
made it through the storm, so it
blasts off

soaring into space
to release a satellite
hoping to keep an eye on North Korea's
future missile experiments.

Jiichan sighs in relief.

AUGUST 29, 2001

LAST BLASTS OF SUMMER

Hanabi, fire flowers,
postponed by the typhoon,
explode in partly cloudy skies
down by the swollen river.

We watch on TV
smiley faces and morning glories and
my favorite, chrysanthemums,
bursting.

After the finale
firecrackers pop, whistle, squeal
in parks, gardens, other neighborhoods.

Papa calls to tell me
to endure my time
at school here
patiently.

I do not want to go to bed,
but I do.
I do not want tomorrow to come,
but it does.
I do not want to wake up,
but I do.

SEPTEMBER 2001

ON TIME

I open the shutters to
the sun

up hours before I wake
it makes me feel late.

When I leave the house,
Mom says,
“Hang in there.”

I leave thinking I would rather stay here
at “Obaachan’s School.”

SCHOOL

In an apartment parking lot,
students and I wait
wearing summer clothes
holding our bags of emergency hoods
and our bags of indoor shoes.

I will be invisible
until I walk into a classroom.
But I see them
look at me
from the corners of their eyes.

First graders in required yellow hats
cluster.
Classmates group.
I stand alone.

A line forms;
two sixth graders lead
one from the front
one from the back.

Mothers in threes
along the street
hold yellow flags at each intersection
reminding drivers
school has started.

Some mothers greet us.
We greet.
Some mothers are statues.
We pass in silence.
We take our cues from them.

Last night, a flag came to the house
with instructions from a PTA member.

Jiichan is on the street,
smiling,
filling in for Mom.

SEPTEMBER 1, 2001

PART OF THE DRILL

At the shoe shelves,
in the hall,
in the classroom,
I'm still invisible.

The boy with cold eyes
from the clump of trees at the broken gravestones is here.

I see now he is big for his age.
Like me.

Teacher introduces me.
Row after row of names is called. For me.
Everyone sees me now
that I have a name.
That big boy's name is Masa.

No time for looking at me,
for troublemaking or for chatting
just time enough for
listening to Teacher's instructions,
crawling under our desks,
covering our heads with our emergency hoods.

I think of Papa on the other side of Tokyo
doing drills with other salarymen.
They practice saving each other.

After the last drill
Teacher leads us (wearing our hoods)
outside to the playground
to hand us over to our moms
after a speech
and a moment of silence at noon
in memory of the big earthquake
on this day in 1923.

Jiichan stands in for Mom again.
We walk his bicycle back.

Mom is napping next to the table.
Obaachan has cold tea and homemade onigiri waiting.
They have already eaten.
Jiichan eats one onigiri and nods off
after a weeklong check of every item
in the emergency shed.

We are all a little more prepared for
the Big One, one like the 1923 earthquake,
scientists say will hit Tokyo again
in the future.

For now, I'm more worried about Masa,
the boy with the cold eyes.

And I have all Sunday to worry about him.

STANDING OUT

One look in the mirror
and I know what happened.

Last night, shutters open,
I moved off my futon
looking for a slice of full moon
and fell asleep.

This morning
my whole right side
is cratered
with the imprint of tatami.

First full day of class I face giggles
and Masa's baby talk at recess
asking me if I know how to use a futon.

Everyone laughs and runs away.

I look kind of funny?
Out of this world?

hahahaha

I understand what you're really saying.

FIRST SCHOOL ASSEMBLY

The principal announces
stranger danger on the streets.
First week "walking to school" groups
become "walking from school" groups too
indefinitely.

My first thought—
Masa won't be in my group!

Second thought—
A chance to make friends.

Third thought—
Yikes! Stranger danger.

We walk along. Looking.
What will we do when we see a dangerous stranger?

I see Jiichan
on his bike following us.
I wait for him in the garden.
He looks tired, but smiles
and points to the sign on his bicycle basket:
MAMA PATROL.

Jiichan is my official mom.

THE SCREAMER

I hand Obaachan a note from school
with an order form for a screamer.

Small but loud
it screams
when the string is pulled.

Teacher suggests we carry it at all times
and move it from bag to bag
schoolbag to cram-schoolbag to soccer bag.
In my case, schoolbag to
errand bag.
Kids are alone on the street after Mama Patrol hours.
I'm not.

But without hesitation or complaint

or a word to Mom,

Obaachan fills out the form
puts it and the money
in the envelope
and stamps it
stone to paper
with the household seal
for everyday expenses.

BAG BY BAG

I am moving
into this school.

I hide my NASA pen
in my desk box.

I hold on to it
at my desk
sitting,
listening,
paying attention.

Without my NASA pen
at the board
in line for lunch or for the toilet
in the music room or in the gym,
I look down
at the scuffs
and the dust
from my old school
on my indoor shoes.

FLOWER HEADS

Group by group
we tape
our English practice papers
to the classroom wall.

Teacher put a circle
next to each correct answer.

Instead of a number score,
she drew
a flower head
at the top.

A complete flower head,
a center spiral with
curly petals all around,
is a full mark.
Less detail,
the lower the score.

My paper
has all circles,
and at the top
a circle spun into a spiral
complete with petals.

I tape it to the wall
stand back to look at my full mark, and

glance at the paper next to mine—
all slashes and at the top
the beginning
of a spiral
and
the name
written in *romaji*,
the roman alphabet—
MASA.

I feel his cold eyes on me
all the way back to my chair.

INVITATION

Sachiko from class
and from my "walking to and from school" group
is free on Tuesdays and Thursdays
from ballet and piano lessons.
She asks me to play
(game players)
in the park
when it's sunny

but I can't

Obaachan says
I shouldn't start anything new.

This is family time.
There is a danger on the street.
Besides, I don't have a game player.

I tell Sachiko, "Let's play at recess."

Later among the papers I stuffed
in my parent-message bag,
I find a permission slip
for swimming class tomorrow.

All night I hope it keeps raining!

CLOUDY WITH A CHANCE OF SWIM CLASS

I ask Mom to sign the permission slip
to say I cannot get into the pool.

Like a school pool card,
it has a checklist: fever
vomiting
colds
scrapes
bug bites
I checked but have no checks
except for
the mosquito bite on my belly
I scratched until it bled.
Mom excuses me.

This is the last swim class of fifth grade.

I do not want to swim at this school
I missed school swim lessons this summer
I am behind.

I would rather sit on a bench
and let them wonder
what is wrong with me.

This is the first time I'm glad
mosquitoes think I'm tasty.

No matter.
All the rain made
the pool too dirty for class.

Sachiko and I have a chance for fun.
We make mud balls at recess.

SCHOOL CLEANUP

Masa's group has brooms.
Sachiko's has dustpans.
Mine has wet *zōkin.*
Sweepers sweep into dustpans,
we follow
washing the floor
dipping our rags
in pails of water.

Masa's not sweeping;
he's zigzagging through brooms
clicking handle to handle
everyone ignoring him.

He runs full steam

my group
parts out of his way

I freeze

he rams my thigh with his broom.

I sink into silence
to the floor.

Everyone sees,
everyone hears

no one listens
no one comes to my rescue
no one does anything,
says anything.

I double in pain
and disappear at my desk
into a spot,
ink black.

No one has hit me before. Ever.
Sachiko tells me to ignore Masa.

BREAKING A RULE

I don't wait
for my "walking to and from" group.

I run headlong
into the garden
to Jiichan,
ready to go on patrol.

Panicked,
thinking stranger danger first,
his eyes
become so sad
seeing and hearing
about the bruise
about Masa.

Three times
he places his hand over the bruise,
throws his hand back saying,
"Pain, pain, fly away!"
like I am a child who has fallen down.

Obaachan hovers at the front door.

"Please don't do anything.
Please don't tell Mom. Or Papa."

Obaachan says nothing
puts on a clean apron
and waits.

One hour. Two.
The gate bell is silent.
No apology is coming.

REACTIONS

"Unacceptable," Obaachan says.
Even an accident requires apology.
She calls the school.

The gate bell dings at dinnertime.
Obaachan is in the wrong apron.

Jiichan stays with Mom at the table.
Teacher bows low to Obaachan
gives apologies
for the late hour
for my bruise
for not knowing.

"Poor thing," she says to me,
wants to see it, and is surprised
by its size. As big as a five-hundred-yen coin.

Obaachan stiffens
then says directly
that it is Masa's mother's place to apologize.

Teacher turns red. "That is not possible."
Obaachan's silence pushes for an apology.
Teacher tries to disappear into the wall,
explains in a small voice,
"It cannot be helped."

"I am sorry," Teacher tells me.
Down close to my face, she says, smiling,
"Tell me first if anything happens."

Obaachan's slippers
scuff
heavier than usual
down the hallway behind me.

I pretend I am asleep when Papa calls.
I would not tell him I am hurt
but
he will hear it

in my voice.

NIGHTMARE

All night
a giant Masa chases me down
the hall with a broom.

Obaachan in her best apron
shuffles
down another hall
taking her time
waiting to ambush him
for an apology.

She has no idea he's a giant Masa.
She cannot see what I see.

I shout out of the nightmare.

Mom wakes
calms me
tells me to try to sleep,

but I don't want to go back to sleep.

And I don't want to go to that school.

FOR SPORTS DAY

On the playground
or in the gym on rainy days
we begin training.

This class, along with half the school,
turns our gym hats
inside out
showing the white sides.
We are the white team.

The red team, the other half of the school,
wears the red side out.

Teacher tells one, two, three students to darken
their names on their gym shirts.
We need to look neat and uniform.

My last name is dark enough
written recently
on two ends of a cotton dish towel

one half pinned to the front
the other half to the back
of this gym uniform borrowed
from the school.

From a distance, I will blend in.

TRAINING

Midmorning,
we change into our gym suits.

We practice the fifth-grade dance routine
and sporting events
and the all-grade relay.
We participate in everything
no matter our skill or speed.

We will win events as a team.

I am a fast runner
which doesn't matter
except that
every year I join the fastest runners
at the end of the relay
for an exciting finish.

After the relay trial run
Teacher says I will be a last runner
and MASA will hand me the baton.

AFTER PRACTICE

Masa grabs, crumples, and tosses
my math homework at me
in front of Teacher.

She ignores him.

My NASA pen is missing.

I cannot tell Teacher.

Personal items aren't allowed
at school.

BEFORE BEDTIME

Curled in the circle of light
from the overhead lamp, we lie
futon to futon
pillow to pillow
face to face.

Mom asks about school.

Her cheeks,
drained of the pink
that flushes when she's happy,
fade into the pillowcase.

Her eyes,
flecked with the yellow
that flashes when she's angry,
drown in their blue.

My heart
in my throat says
lub dub   lub dub   lub dub
in English.

My heart wants to tell her
lub dub   lub dub   lub dub
I am broken
about my missing NASA pen

lub dub   lub dub   lub dub
I am sick
about the missing wish

lub dub   lub dub   lub dub
I am worried
about Masa.

I cannot let Mom hear my heart
for this baby
she cannot be worried or sad or mad.
I stand up and pull the lamp cord.

"The lunch menu looks good," I say.

lub dub   lub dub   lub dub
That is the truth.

SCHOOL LUNCH SCHEDULE

Curry rice
later
this month.

Soon.

The serving lists show
I am not in Masa's group to serve lunch.

That means
    we don't walk together
        pushing the food cart to the classroom.

That means
    we don't serve together
        putting food on plates.

That means
    I will have to go through the line for him to serve me.

My name hasn't been added to the list. Yet.

SPORTS DAY PRACTICE IN THE GYM

I am missing my old school
the most during practice

chatting, laughing, cooperating together as a team.

Masa does not cooperate.

Seeing him run toward me with the baton
is a nightmare
but then
he comes to a dead stop
tosses it
makes me chase the baton bouncing
end over end along the floor.

Teacher tells us, "*ganbatte*,"
"hang in there"
"endure."

I do my best with all my strength to be patient.

Glad it's Friday,
a whole weekend of escape.
I need a break from Masa troubles.

BAD WEATHER COMING

"Eh-ma! Eh-ma!"
I keep walking
away from the schoolyard.

"EM-MA!"

I turn, see
Mom and Jiichan in a taxi
coming from her appointment
smiling
happy to see me.

I give Mom the cold eye.
Her face turns baby-seal white.
She realizes what she has done.

She's put an extra *m* in my name.

I look to see if Masa is around.

The ears of the school
my "walking to and from" group
and possibly Masa
hear her call me
something that sounds like God of Hell.

The eyes of the school
my "walking to and from" group
and possibly Masa
see me turn red.

I hide under my umbrella
like a crab under a stone
but walk straight
through puddles
alone.

A weekend of worry is ahead.

ANNIVERSARY OF WORLD'S TREATY OF PEACE WITH JAPAN

Saturday morning cartoons
then noon news:

fifty-six years ago,
Japan agreed to be friends with the world.

Today fifty years ago
forty-eight nations signed the San Francisco Peace Treaty.

Maybe I can make a treaty with Masa.
I look to the right.
Obaachan sits observing
every chopstick click.

To the left,
Mom ignores
the whole table and TV scene.

I'm stuck in the middle with Jiichan.

It will not be easy to make peace.

The earth quakes and rumbles
the house shivers

windows, doors, walls
books, dishes

rattle
like the seeds inside Papa's lotus pod.

Eyes meet
chopstick clicking
stops

begins again.

The earth shakes them into attention
to one another
for a minute.

SEPTEMBER 9, 2001

GRANDPARENTS DAY IN AMERICA

Dressed, fed, brushed,
I call Grandpa Bob and Nana
before heading out the door

on Monday morning
our tenth,
Sunday afternoon
their ninth

they haven't gotten their card yet.

ON THE WAY TO SCHOOL

No one
in my group
mentions the extra *m*
or my crab face last Friday.
No one teases me

but three members warn me not to walk alone
because of the dangerous stranger.

BOUNCING BATON

Rain
again today
relay practice continues
in the gym.

It is torture.

At least Masa says nothing about God of Hell.

No school tomorrow.
Big rain and winds
from two passing typhoons
are expected.

TYPHOON DAY

Before dawn,
we sit at the TV
the flashlight sits at Obaachan's hand
wind and rain rage.

Later the TV shows
people with umbrellas
struggling on the streets of Tokyo
and
people in rain parkas
standing in line at Disney Sea.
It opened a week ago during typhoon season
and two typhoons are hitting today!

The TV tells us
they are tropical storms, not typhoons
but they sound like typhoons.

Great-Grandfather's palm
grabs at the sky
and other garden trees
bang at the shutters
like they want to come inside.

I want outside!
But I am glad to miss Sports Day practice.

SEPTEMBER 11, 2001

SHUTTERED

I can barely breathe.

This house
dodges wind
left to right
right to left
left to right
like a giant Masa
punching it
pushing its walls
pulling its roof
rattling its shutters
shouting through its cracks.

Sirens blare
airplanes are grounded
trains are stalled
power is lost
(not in this neighborhood).

This giant punches and roars
for hours
before it moves on.

We are exhausted.
Jiichan and I help Mom to bed.

SEPTEMBER 11, 2001

AFTER THE STORM

I slide the shutter slowly, quietly,
so Obaachan will not remind me,
"Letting the night air in
is not healthy."

Shutters slide open
gara gara

one after another
house to house.

Neighbors must like what Mom and I like—
the sparkly air after a typhoon.

Papa calls
to tell me the moon and stars have come out.

I have let in the sparkle
but don't even try to see the sky.

I look at Mom,
sound asleep,
          not enjoying the night air
                    one cricket here
                              one cricket there.

TVs blare

a news flash

the whole neighborhood gasps.

SEPTEMBER 11, 2001

NOT KNOWING

Mom sits straight up.
"What?" she says.
"I don't know."
I scoot across tatami
slide the door to the TV room
but
Jiichan, on the other side,
holds the door in place.

"What?" I say through a crack.
"Good night," he says.

Good night?

I look past him
at the TV screen
at smoke in a clear blue sky.
A lot of smoke
in real time
somewhere.
I don't know
what is happening
so when Mom asks, "What happened?"
I am telling the truth when I say,
"I don't know."

She turns over.

Shutters closed. Eyes closed. I listen.

The TV or the volume is turned off.
The phone rings.
I hear Jiichan say Papa's name and
"Let them sleep."

Jiichan rests the phone receiver
lights the candle and incense
strikes the prayer bowl
and chants to open the gate of heaven.

I don't know what happened.
Mom sleeps; I don't.

SEPTEMBER 11, 2001

STUCK IN A MOMENT

I remember Mom's face
her face before knowing,
pale but rested.
There is always good sleep after a typhoon.

Clearing dishes, Obaachan suggests Mom call Grandpa Bob and Nana.

International call service is overloaded.
Mom is confused
horrified
crushed.

Mom wants to see it,
won't believe it
until the TV is turned on.

Jiichan gently suggests *no*.
Mom insists.

Hours after the world has seen it for the first time
we see planes hitting
smoke fluming
paper drifting.

We watch the towers go down
over and over and over.

They keep showing it
over and over and over.

A dust cloud swallows New York City.

There is more—
a plane went down in Pennsylvania
and
the war department of the United States of America
in Washington, DC
is in flames.

Mom sinks into the floor

I cannot find my breath

Jiichan calls the school
I'm not going.

Breakfast was our last meal in peace.

SEPTEMBER 12, 2001

ASHES, ASHES

Papa cannot get to us.

The world is on alert.

He is at work.

Later I hear Jiichan say to Obaachan
behind closed doors,

"If America falls, we fall."

Rooms are thick with incense,
food tastes like burnt flowers,
Mom will not eat much.

Obaachan tells Jiichan, "No more."

He prays
for the dead
and the living
without incense.

REQUEST

Mom says she will not
speak to anyone
on the phone
except Papa,
Grandpa Bob, and Nana.

Friends call her.
I say,
"Sorry, she can't come to the phone"

in Japanese
in English

they ask if she is okay. I say, *Okay*.

But she sits too close to the TV
like she is trying to get there from here.
She took control of the remote
switching
between cable and local stations.

There is no escape for us
from sounds surrounding us
from images attacking us.

Papa calls.
Mom speaks to him
says she needs to leave.

She knows the world is grounded.
She knows she's grounded
because of this baby.

She knows she has to stay grounded for this baby.

She says she needs
to get out
to go to church
to light a candle.

There is no church

nearby.

MESSAGES TO AMERICA

Many nations quickly say "sorry" to America.

REVELATIONS

Five dead
floods
mudslides
in Japan
after two typhoons thrashed through.

Death and damage reports still unknown
in New York City
in Washington, DC
in Pennsylvania
after planes went through
and down.

People show photos
to the camera
asking us
if we have seen their
son or daughter
sister or brother
mother or father
wife or husband
aunt or uncle
cousin
girlfriend or boyfriend
fiancé
friend

Xerox copies
color photos
with names of the missing
hang on fences
poles
and walls of buildings
still standing.

People have hope.

MORNING NOON OR NIGHT?

Time does not matter anymore.

Grandpa Bob and Nana
call again to see how Mom is
how I am
how we are.

We talk

not about towers
and planes going down or through
but I can hear it in their voices:

towers went down
planes went down
and through.

A foreign attack on American land.

The world has changed for them.

I tell them, "Hang in there."

But here
on the other side of the world
I'm having a hard time
doing that.

I do not feel safe anywhere.

Obaachan asks me
if I will go back to school tomorrow.

I AM NOT GOING TO SCHOOL TODAY

Jiichan calls without asking.

NO COMFORT

Mom will not light a candle
at the family altar or
at the table with me.

She and Papa spend an hour together on the phone.

"The phone bill," Obaachan says. "Ten yen a minute."

Mom's heavy book of poetry,
the one Papa forgets to bring when he visits,
arrives
special delivery.

Obaachan sees it,
thinks it's a Bible,
sighs in relief.

Mom sees it, sighs, says, "Heavenly hurt."
Thinking that's the name of a poem, I open the book.
No one else here can read it to her.

The book is a sound of home. Our home.
The pages crinkle like tissue paper
between my fingers

paper so transparent,
shadows of all the poems appear together.

I can't find "Heavenly Hurt"
but read a few words of another poem aloud
and wish I had practiced reading English more.

So, I say aloud the picture book of poetry I know by heart;
one Mom reads to this baby and used to read to me.

She cannot hear me.

Her doctor visits.
He cannot doctor her spirit.

A SLANT OF LIGHT

I call Nana.
She was a high school English teacher
before becoming a librarian

she'll know "Heavenly Hurt."

Emily Dickinson
#258

Nana knows it by heart
recites it to me
but after I hang up I cannot remember any of it
except
the line "where the meanings are,"
the number of the poem,
and the poet.

I look it up.

From what I understand
it will not make Mom feel better.

HEAVY HEART

My head is a blur,
racing at escape velocity,
the speed needed
to “break free”
from gravity.

Before bed, I open the shutters.

I need the expanse
of space
to empty my heart.

Earth and its atmosphere
cannot contain
my sadness

for America

for Grandpa Bob and Nana
for Mom

or
my fear
of losing this baby.

THIS IS MY MESSAGE TO SPACE

I want to be up and away
like Culbertson, the only American
not on Earth
on September eleventh.

I would cut the cord to Earth,
escape into your silence,
find a different view.

I don't want to see or hear or feel
any more sadness.

LIGHTENING

Mom cannot connect with poem #258
or any poem

she cannot disconnect from the news.
We are surrounded by bad news;

this baby is surrounded by bad news.

I uncover Mom's music player
fast-forward to something upbeat—
the Beatles and post-Beatles
section of the playlist.

I place the earphones on her belly
and push play.

"This baby needs some hope."

Jiichan smiles at me
weakly.

A SHOCK OF YELLOW HAIR

In front of a temple
somewhere in Japan
Martha Stewart is grounded.

No flights to America.

Her head is lowered.
She looks out of place.

Mom, Nana, and I watch her on American TV.
Mom reads to us from her magazines.
Martha Stewart is all about home.

With sunken eyes, quivering chin,
Mom watches her
here.

Jiichan watches Mom.

So sad to see someone so far away from home

now

Obaachan says, "Poor thing."

I will not go to school until Mom is stronger.

ARRANGEMENTS

Jiichan calls the school, information,
then a taxi.
He tells me we are going to church.
I don't tell him
Friday is not church day.

We help Mom to the entry hall.

Obaachan follows, saying, "Not good."

Jiichan helps Mom into outdoor slip-ons.

"Dangerous," Obaachan tells Jiichan.

I can't believe she's complaining.

Jiichan takes Mom's hand,
she leans on his shoulder.
It is the closest I have seen him to anyone.
He supports her

past Obaachan
through the door
past the ladder
through the garden.

Together they bow low
and step through the gate.

A plastic vomit bag
waves in her hand.

REACHING OUT

I follow behind and
turn to look at Obaachan
standing on the porch
under fifty-year-old bonsai.

She says nothing to me.

I plow through the gate.
A neighbor looks at me
over her mail
but says nothing.

Is there nothing to say?

The taxi door opens automatically
like an arm stretching out to help Jiichan with Mom.

The driver asks him, "Is she okay?"

Jiichan tells him she has a plastic bag
just in case.

The driver motions to me to get in the front seat.
My stomach jumps to my throat.

I need a plastic bag of my own.
I've never ridden
in the front seat of a car.

My heart and stomach are already sick
enough.

CHURCH

I've never been in a church.
It is not what I expected.
It is not what I have seen in books
or on TV.
This looks like a classroom.
This is a classroom
at a university.

We step through the door
and we are surrounded

in a hug
like from *Barney and Friends*.

They know immediately what Mom needs;
her whole body melts.

Jiichan and I are stuck in the middle.

I have never even hugged Jiichan.

He does not hug.
He does not melt
only his chin melts
now
into his neck
with his back tilted

observing what is happening
to him.

Mom groans and then cries
cries coming up from so deep,
this baby must be crying with her.

Smashed like on a rush-hour train
among them
I let it be a hug
for me.

I feel grounded
and that feels good.

THE GESTURE

We attend their prayer meeting
returning after dark

outside the gate
in the beams of the taxi's headlights
bouquets
wrapped in florist plastic
sparkle like a shattered stained-glass window.

There is no one to thank

I gather

there are no words to say
how much this means
but I will quietly thank everyone
who makes eye contact
or says "good morning" to me in the days after.

No one may say anything about the flowers.
No one may say anything about the towers.
No one may say anything about the dead.

There are no words to say

how much this means.

JARRED

Our dinner is sitting in front of Obaachan
steaming mad

she unwraps
and stands each bouquet
in the ceramic jar
that held the Tanabata bamboo

and places it in Great-Grandfather's room.

Jiichan says, "Good, eh? Flowers can brighten a room,"

then turns the TV on.

FRIDAY MORNING LIVE IN WASHINGTON, DC, FRIDAY EVENING IN JAPAN

Mom goes back to the TV

to share
the National Day of Prayer and Remembrance
for the Victims of the Terrorist Attacks

with Americans in real-time
with astronauts in the International Space Station

with believers of different religions
outside and inside
America's National Cathedral,

a hall of arches
filled with
cathedral tunes
speeches
and five minutes of a battle hymn.

Across the world, across the universe
people stop for three minutes of silence.

Any comfort for Mom is comfort for this baby.

SEPTEMBER 14, 2001

A NEW DAY

We wake to
the news reports that Japan will assist America in war.

Obaachan switches off the TV,
saying, "Japan surrendered,
agreed to
no
more
war.
Ever."

Japan can only defend itself. By law.

Mom retreats
into headphones and pillows
waiting for Papa.

Today I am stuck
between Obaachan's anger
and Mom's sadness.

SEPTEMBER 15, 2001

RESPECT FOR THE AGED DAY

Obaachan reminds me
she and Jiichan are not “aged” yet.

SHOCK

I see Papa's broken heart
on his face
when he arrives on Saturday

and sees

how sad
how pale
how weak
Mom is.

He calls a taxi to take her to the hospital.

They return hours later
I hear him tell Obaachan
the doctor gave her an IV.

RESPECT FOR PAPA

Obaachan says nothing when
Papa suggests watching the evening news.

Jiichan has control of the remote
again
to keep an eye on news here
and there,
he says.

BETTER REST

Papa sleeps through meals.
Obaachan leaves him alone.

Mom is sleeping more than watching TV.

I am sleeping better while Papa is here too

but I am awake during the day
on guard.

MORE WEIGHT

Heart-crushing
news

from the search of ground zero.

People from many nations have been lost.

A young man from Japan
lost his life in the field in Pennsylvania.

And

I've noticed

American news reporters mention Pearl Harbor a lot.

LET IT BE

I wish Obaachan would stop
telling me to go back to school.

CHRYSANTHEMUM WATER

After evening prayer

Jiichan swats the air
to put out the flame
of the altar candle.
His hand skims
the candlestick
and vase of chrysanthemums.

Both
tumble.

Droplets
bounce
scatter
gather
at his knees.

A flower head
floats;
a smoke stream
sinks.

Jiichan freezes, bowed.

I scramble to get a zōkin
to dab the floor before

Obaachan
snatches the flower
heads to the kitchen
throws it on potato eyes and skins
from dinner preparation.

Jiichan is startled back

the water and flowers gone
he doesn't notice anything happened.

I think Jiichan is watching too much TV.

ALL THAT YOU CAN'T LEAVE BEHIND

Mom is stuck in one section of the playlist.
U2 songs over and over and over.

While Jiichan and Papa watch the ten o'clock news
I phone California, chat for a while before
asking Grandpa Bob,
"How do you forget the bad stuff?"

"You never forget the bad stuff"

he says
he's still learning
to look beyond his worries
to see what needs to be done
to go on.

"It's not easy."

"Papa always tells me *ganbatte*."
I tell him that Mom says it's the same as "hang in there,"
but Papa says it means more:

"to endure with strength
                    with effort
                    with patience."

"I'm sure your Japanese grandparents have had to do that."

I think Jiichan has,
but I don't say
because I cannot say
the same about Obaachan.

That would be saying too much.

Grandpa Bob and Nana have too much to worry about.

BACK IN TRAINING

I go back to school Monday
to do what I need to do
to keep going.

I missed a lot of schoolwork.
I missed curry for lunch.
I missed Sports Day practice.

I have to keep running
doing the best I can
to anticipate Masa's moves.

He does not cooperate.

He says nothing, but I know
while I was gone
he didn't have to pass the baton.

He was the last runner.

HAND TO HAND

A long school day followed by non-stop TV:

A Japanese Ministry of Foreign Affairs team
in North Korea
observes how Japan's rice aid is distributed.

Famine victims express gratitude to the team.

People to people
there is some good news
between North Korea and Japan.

I can't tell how Jiichan feels.
He is too quiet these days.

SEPTEMBER 18, 2001

GONE AGAIN

After three
fourteen-hour work days
with a four-hour bus and train commute

Papa was never really here.

He is worn down
tired and weak

and has to move back home.

Obaachan insisted

for the sake of this baby
we are all weakened

and she says Papa will bring us the flu.

Poor Papa,
he is home
sick.

SEPTEMBER 19, 2001

NOT THE SAME AMERICA

Death can come through the mail.

Someone
put a stamp on poison

and mailed it!

Jiichan is out in the garden
when I return
inspecting each piece of mail
local or foreign
before taking it inside.

Obaachan stands at the door.
Says he is foolish.

Nana says she won't send anything for a while.

A DIFFERENT NIGHTMARE

Alone with the TV

sound off

the sky is falling
crumbling
through space
crumbling
slower than the speed of paper
crumbling
like
ashes
to the ground

white powder rain.

SCHOOL ANNOUNCEMENT

The dangerous stranger was caught
down by the river.
No details.
We weren't even told what he did.

I had forgotten to worry about him.

Teacher tells us to keep our screamers on our bags.

My group decides to keep
walking to and from school together.

"Mama Patrol" continues.

MASA SERVING

I have to stand in line
today
for Masa to serve fish.

He doesn't look at me
so no cold eye
not even the fish's.

I watch him serving.
He seems serious

but then
he slaps my fish
onto
my tray
ugh!

it flops
onto
my indoor shoe
yikes!

and
onto the floor
yuck!

I have a stain on my indoor shoe
to remember
Masa.

There is no ! word for that feeling.

Teacher makes him share his fish.

I want to screeeeam,

NO!

FLIGHT 93

The American Congress
is considering giving
gold medals
to the crew and passengers.

Can a young Japanese man get that?

SEPTEMBER 20, 2001

ANOTHER TYPHOON

School closed
houses shuttered
remote controls gripped

the TV anchorman warns us not to go out.
Howling winds tell us the same thing.

In other news—
today,
September twenty-first,
is International Day of Peace.

Tomorrow is the twenty-first in America.
Peace is moving
around the world
through the time zones
as the date changes.
People in many countries have
events planned.

They are making an effort to find peace.

Jiichan and I light a candle at the altar
for Peace One Day.

A BRIGHT SPOT

Watching the American tribute concert
for heroes of September eleventh,
I am looking beyond the sad faces
to the starlit stage
lights beaming
candles gleaming
strobes streaming.

Midway into the song
sung by a singer in a cowboy hat,
Mom puts my hand on her belly, and
says, “Feel.”

An arm, a leg, a foot?

This baby is responding to
the chords of
John Lennon’s “Imagine.”

Mom sings along
Jiichan and I manage a “you-hoo.”
They look brighter.

This baby is our hope.

SEPTEMBER 22, 2001

SUNBURSTS

Obaachan places two yellow chrysanthemums
at the altar
for the fall equinox.

She gathers the utensils
for the graveyard visit.

I hear Jiichan say we should not go.

Obaachan prepares a dish of salt
for outside the gate.

She tells me to stay here with Mom.
I watch her open her parasol
Jiichan follows behind her.

I wonder if she will help him scrub the stones.

SEPTEMBER 23, 2001

THE FLOWER SACRIFICE

I throw out the last
of the bouquets
and soured water.

I hadn't noticed
when the cicadas stopped singing.

BLUE SKIES

A national holiday
a day off to observe the equinox
a break from the house
Jiichan and I
ride
down by the river.

Open space
and sunshine
make me want to go fast.

SEPTEMBER 24, 2001

LIKE THE FLOW OF THE RIVER

The molasses time of day

sakura leaves

pedal the wind at my feet.

I am going too fast
for Jiichan.

Waiting,
soles on the ground
in leaf drifts, I watch

a constellation,
dark and light
dull and sparkling
deep and shallow,

glide past me—

the river's kimono
of autumn amber sun
flowing.

A dragonfly clings
to waving pampas grass.

MINDLESSNESS

Beside me,
a broken pampas's
feathery head bends.

On one foot
I balance
   snap its stem
   swivel on the seat
to slide it between the seat and fender.

Beyond me,
a mangled spider lily's
withering head bows.

I park to rescue it.

On one knee,
I kneel
      shred its stem
      return to my bike
to thread it through the wires of the basket.

Toward me,
a speeding Jiichan's
frantic head bobs.

I signal him.

Not seeing me
he keeps going.

On both feet,
I rush
  straddle the bike
  push sole to pedal
to catch up with him.

MINDLESS

The pampas flutters behind me,
the fire-engine red lily flashes before me

—I realize I look like a—

Nature Thief!

I pedal faster
hurrying to hide
behind the garden gate

fluttering and flashing

Nature Thief! Nature Thief!

Obaachan shrieks when she sees the pampas and lily,
"You don't take public plants!"

And fumes, "No sensibility."

I know I know I know I think *I was not thinking.*

Jiichan looks more than tired.

RAIN, RAIN, PLEASE STAY

Three days of chasing the baton
under hot, sunny skies
I am not sad to see the rain today.

I hope the sky
rains, rains, rains
until Sports Day
and
makes us hold it in the gym

where there's no room for families
and the relay will be short and quick.

The forecast calls for
mostly sunny days
until the end of October.

Dark days ahead.

SEPTEMBER 28, 2001

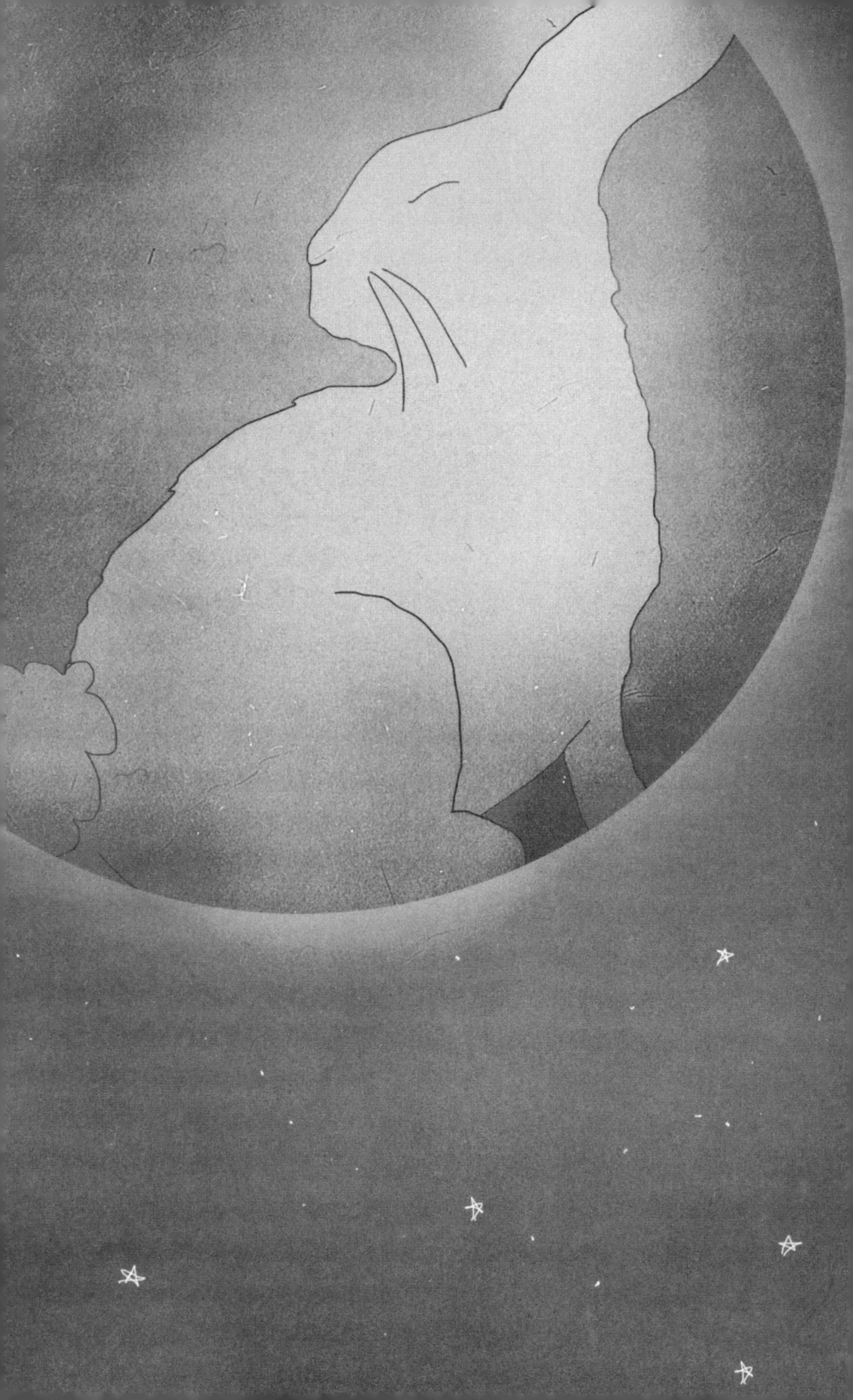

OCTOBER 2001

MINDFUL

Masa cannot sit still
in class

he gets up
goes to the pencil sharpener
goes to the toilet
goes to the playground
on his own
when it's not the appointed time.

Teacher watches his every move
but says nothing to him.
He would keep her busy.

Keeping an eye on him
makes me tired.

He slows me down.

MOON-VIEWING WEEK

Pounding rice into *mochi*
was a favorite time
for me

now
I watch closely
while Masa takes his turn
with the mallet.

He is skillful at pounding.

We all have a hand
in pounding
until the rice is glutinous and ready
to roll into small balls.

To celebrate the beauty of the moon
up closer to the moon
in Papa's room

I place my three small mochi from school
and a pampas stem I bought
with my last year's New Year's money.

White fluff from the pampas
and gnats from the window
cling to the mochi.

Even though I don't have
a clear view of the moon,

I am looking beyond my worries.

OCTOBER 1, 2001

LOOKING FORWARD

Ghibli Museum opened today
just a short bus ride away.

I'd like to fall
into the arms of my neighbor,
Totoro,

but it could take years.

Long lines
everywhere tickets are sold
make it like winning the lottery.

I like to think
of him
minutes away,
a lotus leaf on his head,
waiting.

OCTOBER 1, 2001

DREADING

Sports Day
a national holiday
on a Monday

gives Papa two days off in a row!

Obaachan insists Mom should not go.
Jiichan says he will carry the garden chair for her.

"We will go by taxi," Papa says.
"Mom needs something fun."

Everyone will know she's my mother.
No one goes to Sports Day by taxi.

ANTICIPATING

I am still hoping for bad weather.

Jiichan made a *teru teru bōzu*
(Mom says it's a Kleenex ghost)
and hung it in the window
to wish for fair weather.
We watch the clouds
and the weather report.

Scattered showers, Sports Day will go on.

Obaachan started cooking early
delicious foods
to eat for breakfast and

to fill the *obentō* boxes
for the family
to eat on the sidelines
and for me
to eat in the classroom.

The class is interested in mine:
wiener cut like octopus
sweet egg
broccoli
grilled fish
onigiri

tomato
all sitting on a lettuce leaf.

Mine is the best looking obento, they say.
I savor each bite
like it's my last meal.

OCTOBER 8, 2001

RELAY

One after another,
students take turns to sit, stand,
run the course,
pass the baton.

"Ob-la-di, ob-la-da"
the Beatles song
looping

"Ob-la-di"
I sit behind Masa
waiting

"Ob-la-da"
he digs his heels into the muddy dirt
not watching
not cheering
not caring?

I look toward Mom.
Jiichan is holding an umbrella over her.

She loves this event.
They play this song every year at my school.

She's not singing along today,
but she looks okay

holding her belly;
this baby must be moving to the beat.

“Life goes on”

Masa’s time to stand
take his mark, ready, set, go.

I am on my mark

to take my turn.

"LA-LA, HOW THE LIFE GOES ON"

Masa runs toward me
slaps
the baton
into my hand
for the first time

I'm off
running
head down and fast

skidding
I slide
reaching across
the finish line
first.

The white team, our team, gets the point!

Mom is standing, worried.
I wave.

Scuffed up but not skinned up
I spend the last event
at the nurses' tent
being dabbed with alcohol.

I watch
the red team in a line passing a big red ball

the white team in a line passing a big white ball
over their heads toward a goal
remembering Teacher's advice:
"Keep your eye on the ball and
be mindful of others."

Sports Day ends in a tie.
Later, Mom congratulates me.
Obaachan mentions it was a team effort.
Papa says, "Well done, Ema."

Jiichan comments on the sweet olive-tree blossoms.

Before Papa leaves, he asks me to watch over Mom.

OCTOBER 8, 2001

AMERICA INVADES AFGHANISTAN

During the evening news,
Obaachan takes the remote control
away from Jiichan
switches off the TV
and says,

"No more."

We will not watch a war.

DRAFTED

Jiichan has to participate
on the school's fall festival committee.
He says the festival sounds fun.

I have to go since
Jiichan has to work so hard.

But I don't want to go.

What would be a good excuse?

BABY IN DANGER

Mom sits up in bed
holding her belly
breathing quickly
chanting deeply

whoosh, whoosh
get Jiichan
whoosh, whoosh
get Jiichan
whoosh, whoosh

GET JIICHAN!

Stumbling
in the darkness
in the telephone cord
in the middle of the TV room
I shout,
"Ji-i-chan!"

Scramble
slide
crash
he appears at my feet

pulls the phone cord

dials
calls a taxi.

The baby is coming

almost two months
early.

DROPS OF JUPITER

Jiichan has control of
the hospital lobby TV

tuning into reports of

NASA's *Galileo* sailing

by a moon of
Jupiter,
the closest encounter ever,

and
the US Navy
searching the *Ehime Maru*
in shallow waters near Honolulu.

Obaachan and I circle
each other
in opposite directions
around the lobby.

I keep an eye on her
and with each step wonder
why
this baby is in a hurry.

Obaachan stops to read notices on the bulletin board.

I orbit past her
wishing
there were any way
on Earth

to stop this baby from coming early.

OCTOBER 16, 2001

FALSE ALARM

But this baby doesn't come

and keeps us there
waiting
for Papa to arrive
before the doctor
sends us all back
with instructions to
keep Mom comfortable and

calm.

RESTLESS

Hard to concentrate on
the homework assignment
Sachiko dropped in the mailbox.
I check on Mom every thirty minutes.

Obaachan says I cannot miss any more school.

I don't know how
I will make it through
tomorrow
away from Mom.

I tell Jiichan to watch over her,
but I know I don't have to tell him that.

BEHIND

I already missed too much
last month.

Yesterday I missed
the beginning of art projects
for the exhibition at the end of November.

Everyone has planned
the first project:
a painting to celebrate the Sun.

I am behind in art!

CONCENTRATION

I begin to sketch

a smaller circle
on top of a bigger circle
evolves into—
Mom.

The bigger circle is her belly—
this baby,
the shining Sun.

The idea grows
involving
two more smaller circles;
a smaller circle
on top of a larger circle
revolving
Mom and the Sun—

Me.

I only outline.

Masa seems to like art.
He is seriously planning an exploding Sun.

PEACE ON EARTH

This baby gives us another scare.
The doctor sends us back.

Jiichan and I
pile into the backseat of a taxi with Mom
Papa sits up front
Obaachan goes back by bus.

"Radio okay?" the driver asks
in the most polite language.

Jiichan says yes and leans in;
the TV has been off
for more than a week.

The radio tells us,

after peace talks, the Irish Republican Army
is laying down its guns.

We all cheer,
even the driver.

I hope this good news spreads
from Ireland
east
across the Middle East

across the Far East
west
across the West
across the world, and
across the universe
for international peace one day
soon.

Thank you, Baby!
We wouldn't have heard the news
without your alarm.

At bedtime, I say to Mom's belly, to this baby,
"I can't wait, but please don't hurry!"

OCTOBER 24, 2001

NAMING

Now or later,
this baby needs a name.

Still, no one has mentioned possibilities
and
no one is talking about finding any.

Not sleeping,
lying in night light
monitoring Mom's breathing,
I see possibilities

in her collage.

I tiptoe into the TV room.
Obaachan is soaking in the bath
Papa is snoozing on the floor
Jiichan is sneaking a look at the news.

No one sees me with the collage
pulling a book of baby names from a shelf,

no one sees me
looking up the kanji possibilities for the words, and

no one sees me
circling two words on Mom's collage.

I am the one who finds a name,
a perfect name,
for this baby.

GONE AND COMING

Papa went back and forth
to work
from here
waiting for this baby.

This baby waits

until he is far away on a business trip

then decides to come.

IN NO TIME

I jump to my feet
scrambling
for the phone cord
coming out of restless sleep
Mom crumples into a ball
groaning.

This time is different
she does not whoosh or chant.

Jiichan!

He phones for an ambulance.

"We need to go," Mom whispers.

Ten minutes we are out the door
two steps, cringe, two steps, cringe
through the gate
we advance toward the main street to flag
any taxi that comes along.

An ambulance slows, stops,
the driver shouts "Satoh-san?"
Jiichan flags him with "Yes!"

They are gone
and I am alone with Obaachan.

I don't understand.
I always go with Mom.
Obaachan tells me I need rest.

WIDE AWAKE

I lie alone in Great-Grandfather's room
thinking
I won't sleep tonight
tomorrow is Saturday

why am I here?

Burning incense reaches my nose.
Obaachan is praying.

I don't sleep. Much.

At breakfast I see
she has made an obento for Jiichan.

He has not called.

I am hoping this baby listened to me and did not come early.

ARRIVAL

Jiichan greets us,
instructs us
to wash hands
with disinfectant
and to put on masks
from dispensers in the hallway.

He says nothing.

A nurse tells us
Mom is too weak to see us,

but shows us this baby
wrapped in a pink towel
in a glass box.

Little Sister!

has a face.

Little Sister!
(I can say it out loud)

has black hair
and is dark. Red.

Little Sister!

doesn't look like me at all;
she is small
but is big for her age.
Just like me.

OCTOBER 27, 2001

SOMETHING WRONG?

Little Sister does not cry
or open her eyes.

I get close to the glass
say her name

the name I found

—*Miki*—

with kanji
"mi" from *mirai,* future
"ki" from *kibō*, hope

"future"   "hope"

I see her uncurl 1-2-3 fingers.

She likes it!

Obaachan says nothing.

Jiichan's eyes sparkle

with tears.

OBAACHAN'S ORDERS

On the bus, Obaachan tells me
to go back with Jiichan to help start dinner.

She heads for the shrine to pray for Little Sister and Mom.

JIICHAN'S PRAYERS

The house is thick
with worry
with incense
with prayers.

Little Sister and Mom are weak

I hear Jiichan say
behind closed doors

they have to stay a long time
in the hospital.

Obaachan says nothing
about the expense.

I reach for one of Mom's plastic bags.

My heart wants to throw up
but my stomach won't.

A ROOM TO MYSELF

I toss
and turn
in bed

tossing
I see Mom falling
into the TV

turning
I see Mom whooshing
in bed

tossing
I see Mom lying
in a hospital bed

turning
I see Little Sister lying
in a glass box

tossing
I see my blue-sky wish
floating
toward the stars.

CREAM & RUM RAISIN COOKIES

Jiichan bows over a box
wrapped in a deep purple *furoshiki.*
The head nurse takes it
from his outstretched arms
and later, bowing, returns the silk cloth
folded.

In line for hours
outside the pastry shop
way downtown
he bought the best for the hospital staff.

"So they will give your mother
and Little Sister the best care."

Obaachan says nothing
about the expense. In front of me.

Behind closed doors she mentions
hospital costs and the price of funerals.

OCTOBER 28, 2001

RUSHING

On a *shinkansen*
outside Tokyo
Papa hurries

to meet Little Sister.

ALONE WITH MOM AND PAPA

Mom is weak
whiter than pale
says nothing except
not to worry about her.

I hold out her collage
in front of her and Papa
and whisper the name I chose
for Little Sister.

Mom smiles.
Papa does too.

They like it. And so does Little Sister.
That's what matters,
I hope.

WORRIED

Nana and Grandpa Bob call to say
they are coming.
Jiichan
and Obaachan are already worrying.

Jiichan is worried about bedding.
"Can they sleep on a futon?"

Papa says they can sleep anywhere any time.

Obaachan is worried about food.
"Wasting money on things they won't eat."

Papa says they will eat anything.

Papa says they are coming
to see Mom and meet Little Sister.
Nothing else matters.

Nana and Grandpa Bob are worried about flying.
They don't say so
but I know so.
Everyone is

after seeing planes go through buildings
and down in a field
on September 11.

BREATHLESS JIICHAN

Obaachan makes a list

> 1) Check least raggedy
> towels, sheets

A few new towels are needed.

"What kind of pillow would Americans like?" Jiichan asks.

Obaachan says, "Guests can't complain."

> 2) Air the futon and pillows.

The sun is not hot enough.
Sending them out costs too much.
Jiichan suggests buying a futon fluffer.
Obaachan tells him we don't need that.
"They will not notice."

> 3) Buy new pajamas that are presentable for guests to see.
> Everyone agrees.

> 4) Scrub the bath, clean the tatami and kitchen.

The house is filled with chemical cleansers and incense.

It is not easy to prepare for living, breathing guests.

OCTOBER 28, 2001

EXHAUSTED

Papa has to be gone again

and left before I got up for school.
I will stick to Jiichan.

OCTOBER 29, 2001

SUN'S OUT

Before leaving for school,
I watch Jiichan pull
futons and blankets
out to air and
hear Obaachan push
him
with instructions
and complaints.

Poor Jiichan.

He has a long shopping list too.

At school Masa still eyes me.

I look up
over his head.

My faceless Sun painting
radiates from high
on the wall
among the others.

I am glad to know my little sister's face,
but I am worried she came early.

BEYOND WORRY

Jiichan's not on Mama Patrol.

I slide the gate

and find him
collapsed over his bicycle

eyes closed, mouth open,
his skin is fish cold, fish white.
I kneel beside him, slap his hand.
A pink print of my hand surfaces.

I pull my screamer
Obaachan comes running.

I scream,
"One-one-nine! One-one-nine!"

She runs back inside.

Sirens stretch from a distance
growing, coming down the main street
slowing, turning into our street
pounding, barging into the houses.

Men in uniform and crash helmets
rush toward the open gate

a stretcher between them
the man in front bends
the man in back bumps
through the gate
almost pushing it down.

A man on radio waits in the ambulance.

"I opened the gate
and found him like this."

BEYOND KNOWING

They need to know what happened
to know where to take him.
"I don't know what happened."

One man asks for his insurance card
Jiichan mumbles
Obaachan, standing over us, motions to his wallet.

The man slips it
and my boshi techo
from Jiichan's back pocket
hands them to me
I find the card inside
and watch my hand
give it to the man.

They decide on a hospital
bow over Jiichan
carrying him on the stretcher
through the gate toward the ambulance.

Obaachan tells them she will meet them there.

The ambulance door closes.
I can't see Jiichan anymore.
Breath is knocked out of me.
I balance on Obaachan.

I look up at her.
She lets me go with Jiichan,
saying she will meet me there.

Flashing and wailing
the ambulance turns
in the direction opposite
of Little Sister and Mom.

I am alone with Jiichan in the back
I pat his hand
clutching my boshi techo and his insurance card
in my other hand.

I am alone in the waiting room.
No one else is there.
Obaachan arrives with his new pajamas,
the new towels, and a box of tissues.

"In case he needs to stay overnight."

BEYOND REASON

What happened to Jiichan?
An attack? A stroke?

running tests

nothing we can do

we should leave

I realize
I could be alone with Obaachan
for a long time.

I don't remember dinnertime
I don't remember bath time

I remember Papa saying on the phone
he will be here tomorrow evening.

THE HOUSE TO OURSELVES

I don't want to sleep
next to Mom's empty futon
downstairs

I want to be up and away . . .

While Obaachan is in the bath,
I carry Mom's pillow upstairs
pull a guest futon from the closet
and lie down.

Tears stream from the corners of my eyes
soaking my hair,
my ears, and her pillow.

Jiichan is weakened
Mom and Little Sister are weakened
I am weakened.

Obaachan comes up the stairs
slides open the door to check on me
I pretend I am asleep
she leaves me alone

I bury my face in Mom's pillow
afraid
sick

and lonely
having any room
to myself.

A DAY IN THE LIFE

Without Jiichan and Mom in the house
silence
hurts my heart.

At four a.m. I move to the TV room.

Obaachan is not up yet.

Will she make me go to school?

I hear her blankets ruffle
then the closet door slide;

startled to see me
she says good morning
on her way to the laundry room.
She is going through the motions
of a normal day.

She calls the school.
We are going to the hospital
to see Jiichan.

WHAT NEEDS TO BE DONE TO GO ON

Jiichan's heart, the doctor tells us,

needs to rest
needs less stress
needs a stay
in the hospital.

FOR JIICHAN

Obaachan leads me down
the narrow street
that Mom calls "Angel Street"
because of a pronunciation mistake
she made on her first visit here

where
life goes on
chattering and clattering
eating and drinking
buying and selling
along
the way
to the shrine
near Obaachan's neighborhood station.

At the foot of the *torii*,
the gate between street and shrine,
we bow low, once,
and enter the grounds
shaded by the city's oldest trees.

At the basin, we ladle cold water
left hand, right.

I watch and follow Obaachan's lead
tipping the ladle to clean the handle

(Something I've never done before).

She hands me my handkerchief from her bag.

Standing before the hall,
she hands me a coin to throw.

I clap before she doesn't.

Ignoring my mistake,
she bows twice, throws a coin,
pulls the thick rope with two hands,
claps twice.
I am a beat behind her,
but we pray together, until
she bows once

I follow.

She buys a wooden tablet
writing, asking, wishing
for good health for Jiichan.
Her request
hangs on the frame
underneath the oldest shrine tree
and tap, tap, taps against
others.

A breeze?
An earthquake?
An angel lifting them to read?

Back on the street,
shop to shop,
Obaachan buys grilled chicken on sticks,
octopus puffs, and discounted obento for our dinner,
fussing about the price of things.

FOR PAPA

A short workday.

A visit
with Jiichan's doctor
with Little Sister's doctor
with Mom's doctor.

A visit
with Jiichan
with Little Sister
with Mom.

The hospitals let him stay long after visiting hours

before he takes the last trains
and busses
across Tokyo
home.

FOR MOM AND LITTLE SISTER

Time in the hospital
to get stronger.

The pile of money
Mom thinks Obaachan is sitting on
is getting closer and closer
to the ground
day by day.

This is what
Obaachan saved for.

FOR OBAACHAN

Nana and Grandpa Bob call
telling me to say how sorry they are

to Obaachan
and to Jiichan when I see him.

They ask if there is anything they can do.

They will not visit.

FOR ME

Back at school
I look up at my Sun painting
wishing I could add
Jiichan next to me
holding hands.

OCTOBER 31, 2001

FOR JIICHAN'S NURSES

On our way to the hospital
we buy almond crisp cookies
from the department store near the station.
Inexpensive,
shaped like leaves,
they are seasonal and popular.

So sad

Jiichan knows
no one can go
all the way into Tokyo
to buy cream and rum raisin cookies
"for the best care"
for him.

BEHIND CURTAIN 6

In the corner
by the window
Obaachan slides back the curtain
at the end of Jiichan's bed.

We're both startled.
Jiichan, too.
He's sitting on the side of the bed
attached to an IV.

He says he is on his way to the toilet.

"Not good," Obaachan says
slaps her hand to his forehead
and keeps it there.

She is checking his temperature.

Fever.

He wants to go to the toilet alone.
She doesn't let him have his way.

Something has to change.

FOR US ALL

After just one week
two emergencies
two ambulance rides
hours of waiting
and worrying

I realize what day it is.

I scoop and eat
the insides of my dessert,
a whole persimmon,

and cut with a toothpick
triangles for eyes
and a slit for a mouth,
a scary face.

From the altar I get
a one-minute prayer candle
and light it inside the persimmon
and tell Obaachan,

"Americans make these
jack-o'-lanterns
from pumpkins

to scare away demons."

Obaachan asks if this persimmon will work.

"I hope so."

OCTOBER 31, 2001

HORROR

In bed I realize I missed the midterm tests.
Teacher didn't mention a make-up test today.

NOVEMBER 2001

GIFTS

The Grandparents Day card
finally makes it to Nana and Grandpa Bob.

It came at the right time

they tell me

the card
and all the stamps brighten their days.

Something is coming for me, they say.
Teacher said nothing about making up the midterm.

NOVEMBER 1, 2001

NEXT BEST THING

A package of stars,
plastic ones that glow in the dark,
arrives from Grandpa Bob and Nana.

While Obaachan is out on errands,
I pull the step stool
into Great-Grandfather's room
where Mom and Little Sister and I will stay together.

I am still too short to reach the ceiling.

I get the long-handled shoehorn
peel a star from the paper
place it on the tip
climb the step stool
and stick the star to the ceiling.

In the afternoon light
it looks a little messy
but at night
the starry, starry
ceiling brightens the room.

I wish I had put them upstairs
where I am sleeping now

but while Obaachan bathes

I sit under the starry ceiling
and wait for Little Sister
and Mom.

SOMETHING FOR JIICHAN

At breakfast I tell Obaachan I want
to brighten Jiichan's hospital room
with flowers from the garden.
I don't ask to spend money.

Cosmos are finishing their bloom.

Obaachan looks disappointed in me.

"A flower might disturb his roommates."

Disturb?

"Allergies," she says. "You must think of others."

HEARTACHE

In music class,
my brain is out of sync
I am not getting the fingering
of a tune on the *pianika*.

Masa isn't either.

He gets up
grabs a mallet
and clinks the length
of the xylophone.

Teacher instructs him
to sit down
at his pianika
like the rest of us.

Three times through the song I can play it by heart.

Two p.m.
futon swatting
keeps the beat with us.

Throughout the day
back at home
balcony by balcony
futon pounding

echoes

the heartbeat of the neighborhood

I could feel in my chest

there

stronger than

here

my heart is weakened

choking back tears for Jiichan's heart.

BANDAGING

Choosing yogurt-drink cups
                    bandages
                    boxes
                    wire
                    straws, and
using paste and paints and clay
we construct art project number two.

Sachiko wraps bandages
                around
                yogurt-drink cups
building a wobbly tower.

I cannot think what to do with a strip of bandage soaked in watered-down paste.
My wish for better skill in crafts has not come true.

I wrap this way
that way
it takes shape

of a heart.

I paint it purple.

I can't tell what Masa is making.

BRIGHTENING JIICHAN

Wish I knew how to make origami flowers.
Jiichan taught me to make cranes
before nursery school.
I told Obaachan I wanted to make one thousand cranes for Jiichan.

"He'll think we're not telling him something."

He will think he is sicker than he is.

So while the paint is drying
on my bandaged heart
I make one crane
pierce it
with a straw
stick it in a piece of clay at the bottom
of an empty yogurt-drink bottle.

Jiichan says "American ingenuity"
when he sees it.

His eyes sparkle over his mask.

HAND TO LIPS

A squeaky cart stops outside Jiichan's room
a nurse sets dinner
tray by tray
behind six curtains.
The coughing patient in the opposite corner
says he doesn't need it.

Jiichan's not interested
in the rice, miso soup,
stewed chicken and vegetables.

He was doing better on the IV.

Obaachan picks up the miso soup
holds the plastic bowl to his lips—
lips that asked her to marry him by saying,

Will you make me miso soup?

the old way of asking to spend a lifetime together

making miso soup
as long as they both shall live.

For the first time since they married
someone else is making his miso soup.

A MATCHED PAIR

Mom and I usually send presents early
to Grandpa Bob and Nana
to avoid the Christmas mail rush.

Obaachan digs through her closet
presents
a choice of three
unopened boxed sets
of his-and-hers handkerchiefs
stashed away for emergency gift-giving
saying
we will wrap and mail them
on our way to the hospital.

I choose the dark blue and pink flowered handkerchief set.
Of the three, that is the one I think they may like.

But I have never seen them use handkerchiefs.

Today is a national holiday.

Obaachan forgot Culture Day!

She cannot send them until Monday.

UNDER THE ROCK

A list of
things for me to do
things for me to get
things for me to clean
waits for me
on the shoe cabinet
after school.

Obaachan forbids me to ride my bike.
She will not budge.

She says one bad thing can lead to another.
Especially when you're worried.

Keeping busy does not stop
my worries.
It only makes me tired.

Falling asleep
doing my homework,
I fall even more behind.

Obaachan nods off
during my nightly reading assignment.

She is starting to crack.

LOSING GROUND

No flower heads
at the top of my papers,
I sit in at recess
to catch up on math
and kanji.

Never behind,
I've always stayed ahead
to show I know
double what teachers think
I should know.

Teacher gives me
a metal ring
with small blank flash cards
dangling from it
and shows me the kanji to copy.

"Practice where you go," she says.

She knows I spend a lot of time
on buses and trains.
(I told her our family matters.)

I am not sure my brain can keep up with flash cards.

STRETCHED

Too many chores,
too much homework,
too much catch-up,
I cut corners.

Obaachan takes the time to notice.

She yells at me
clenched teeth, muffled voice
so neighbors can't hear
that I am using the inside broom outside.

I have been saving steps all week
instead of
getting the proper broom from the shed.

Obaachan will really be mad
if she climbs the stairs and sees
I don't put the futon in the closet every morning.

MINDFULNESS

But like Jiichan
I give each plant
one after
one tin cup
full of water.

A hose would be easier, faster
but
I see what he sees
in watering

slower

drizzling gives me time
to notice leaves
holding sunlight

to see leaves
holding sunlight

to enjoy leaves
holding sunlight

I climb the ladder
step by step
into Jiichan's world

until Obaachan pulls me down to Earth.

FUTURE HOPE

I talk to Grandpa Bob and Nana
about Miki
using Miki's name
Miki this,
Miki that.

Obaachan doesn't understand English.

She doesn't say anything
after I hang up.

SILENT TREATMENT

Over
the crackle and buckle
of plastic takeaway boxes
we picked up for dinner,
I ask to turn on the TV.

Obaachan nods; I search for a comedy
but find the news.
Ground zero cleanup continues.

Thousands of people are missing in America.

Ehime Maru recovery ends.

One high school student is still missing at sea.
His bones will not join his family
under their gravestone.

"So sad families are apart."

No response. Why?
Using the wrong broom? Naming Little Sister?

Tonight, the coldest night so far,
I soak in the hot bath
too long.

Obaachan is tired and

not pleased.

I scramble under blankets
to capture the bath heat.
Cold is a weight
like heat.

No sunny room
no heaters
no place to get warm
except the bath and under blankets,
I am wondering which is worse
cold or hot
silence or fussing.

NOVEMBER 8, 2001

OUT OF THIS WORLD

Night and day
Miki sleeps
in a glass box
except when Mom is feeding her.

Night and day
Mom feeds Miki
talks to Miki
reads to Miki.

(I like to say *Miki.*)

They are in their own world
together.

Miki doesn't open her eyes
when I read or talk to her
through a mask
and the glass,
but her mouth moves.
It's funny.

Being with them
is like being on vacation
from the world.

There is a gray phone
for international calls
in the lobby.
Mom calls Nana and Grandpa Bob once in a while.

They need a vacation from the world too.

GOING ON

The TV in Jiichan's hospital lobby
reports it is an American holiday,
Veterans Day, November eleventh,
to remember the soldiers after World War I.

A day now to remember
all soldiers of all
America's wars.

It is also the birthday
of the *Ehime Maru* Memorial Association.

A memorial will be built to remember the boys and men.

What is needed to go on—

to remember.

This news is not so stressful,
but I don't tell Jiichan.

Instead I tell him
Grandpa Bob called to report
comet debris will hit the Earth's atmosphere
with a light show
next week
from

two a.m. to four thirty a.m. Tokyo time.

Eight thousand meteors per hour!

Then I realize Jiichan won't be able to see it from behind this curtain.

NOVEMBER 12, 2001

ELEVATION

Under Mom's pillow,
the alarm clock beeps.
So cold I don't want to get up
I pull on my coat under the blankets,
tiptoe through and out
up the ladder to
the roof of the porch
to watch the light show.

No one else is out.
Maybe it's on TV.

From above,
astronauts keep watch.
From below,
I watch the trailing light
between us.

Looks like stars
are falling from the sky

but it is just a comet
falling in pieces.
No constellations are changing.

I make a wish anyway
that everything will be all right

and remember
Robert Louis Stevenson's "Happy Thought":

The world is so full of a number of things
I'm sure we should all be as happy as kings.

After the towers went down,
Mom could not hear me recite it by heart.
Now Jiichan has lost heart.
To be "as happy as kings" is not so easy,

but I fill my heart with this sparkling treasure
hoping to push out the ache.

NOVEMBER 19, 2001

THE EARTH QUAKES

I'm dreaming
I am nightmaring
the floor, windows, walls
rumble
shudder
tremble

like Godzilla is walking up to the gate

tremble
shudder
rumble

I'm not nightmaring!

I scramble
slide the door
look to see
the porch light shining
on Obaachan's face
at the foot of the stairs.

We look at each other
and step back into shadows.

At the hospital
Jiichan tells me

he didn't feel the earth move
but, from the lobby window,
he saw some stars fall.

Obaachan is not pleased.

Jiichan is supposed to rest.

AFTER SCHOOL

Coins and a note
on the shoe cabinet
tell me
Obaachan is spending the whole day
at the hospital with Jiichan
and
for me
to visit Mom and Little Sister.

ON MY OWN

I take the bus
to visit Mom and Little Sister
studying flash cards
on my lap
under my errand bag
(I don't want anyone to know I need help).

Mom is walking
looking healthier
stronger
wondering where Obaachan is.

I tell her
hand her mail
and
change the subject to

"This baby sleeps a lot."

Her eyes are always closed.

"Miki is growing stronger," Mom says, beaming.

Miki? Really?

Mom shows me the copy of registration papers
Papa filed at our city office

naming this baby, Little Sister,
the name I found
on my own.

TIME TOGETHER

Mom has two hot canned teas waiting.
We sit beside Miki's glass box.

Mom chats about
her visitors,
her phone calls,
her meals;
she asks about
Jiichan,
my class,
my time alone with Obaachan.

I can't tell her much.

I watch Miki
grow stronger
while sleeping
until Mom says,
"It's time to go."

I say good-bye
reaching a disinfected finger
toward Miki.

Her fingers curl one, two, three
around it.

Mom squeezes me
gets my sugar
and says,
"I am sorry we're not ready to go with you."

"Me too."

WRONG TURN

To the bus stop
I take a street
lined with gingko trees.

Leaves,
heavy like paper plates,

clink clink

from branches

paving the sidewalk
with gold.

I click my heels in dance steps
I would never do with Obaachan.

MARCHING

Obaachan returns
plods through the hall
stands over me
leads me
to the entry hall

and
motions to my shoes.

I know
to take time
to turn them
toes to the door
after I enter.

My shoes' toes are facing the door.

I look up at her.

She shifts
into mad.

A deep breath tells me—
gingko fruit!

Stinky like vomit.

I tracked in
more work
for myself.

Scrub these shoes!
Scrub the floor!
Scrub the stone path!

Good thing I am used to the smell of vomit.

FLIGHT

Cloaked in gray coats
capped in black berets
magpies

flick
silver tails and
sky-blue wings

swing
electrical wires

pick
Great-Grandfather's palm

flick
swing
pick

twittering
same notes
same notes
same notes
flick
swing
pick

tittering
twittering
teetering
between earth and sky.

I enjoy them from Papa's window.

Obaachan bolts from the front door
shouts and shoos
them away with the garden broom
I had left in the entry hall.

ALONE ON ERRANDS

I am watching my step
more than ever
everywhere I go.

From the clump of trees,
Masa pounces
my heart flops

I squeal like a mouse under a cat's paw.

He laughs
dances like a demon
and tosses something at me . . .
a cicada shell.

Dazed,
then tuned in,
I watch him and think,
Someone needs to throw salt on him.

I look beyond him, ignore
his dancing
his rattling hands in front of my face.

He starts calling me God of Hell.
I ignore him, but
his fingertips graze my cheek.

I slap slap slap at his arms,

and scream,
"For sure I am God of Hell! Watch out!"

He steps backward.
I step forward,
crushing the cicada shell under my shoe, and shout,
"I will spirit you away!"

I charge him
grab his arm
pull.

My aggression is stunning.

He pulls free,
scrambles, runs.

Now who's the bully?

INSTANT KARMA

I stomp to the shops.
I march back
realizing at the gate
I forgot to buy tea.

Just let Obaachan say something about that!

I will *not* walk
all the way back to the shop

to buy tea.

Obaachan is still not talking to me
even after unpacking the groceries.

I miss the hot cup of tea at dinner.

ON THE BUS WITH OBAACHAN

Standing, tired after hospital visits,
I know what she is thinking:
Younger generations don't give up
their seats for their elders
these days.

Obaachan is fuming
but she isn't showing anything
but manners.

We are standing over
a man cutting his nose hair.

The bus jostles.

I can barely stand

Obaachan not saying anything
not even looking at him
even from the corner of her eye.

Manners.

Obaachan seems smaller outside the house.

These days, I am not so sure
I am the same person
anywhere I go.

THE WORST NIGHTMARE

I am the giant chasing Masa.

GROUNDING

Our class
snakes along the street
heads toward the river
to a small field.

Masa is sticking to the farmer
studying his every move
as he instructs us how to
pull *daikon*.
Two groups form.

Masa's group pulls.
Most struggle to free
the long, thick radishes
from the soil.
The farmer tells Masa
"Good job!"
Masa is happy.

My group sits
waits
snaps off the tops.
We all have green fingertips.

Today is our civic lesson

for appreciation.

The farmer thanks us
tells us to fill the plastic bags
we brought from home
with the greens.
Back at school we divvy up
the leaves to make sure
everyone gets a fair share.

Obaachan seems pleased to receive it
even though it is a muddy mess.

Before her first bite, she says,
"Itadakimasu."

She says it at every meal but
today it is the first time in a week
she says something in my direction.

Papa has always translated itadakimasu as

"Thank you, farmers!"

THANKSGIVING

Papa has a day off
Labor Thanksgiving, giving thanks to workers!

Mom and Papa and I celebrate
America's Thanksgiving on this day.

This year, because of the time difference,
they're on the same day.
Papa will spend the day with us.

This year will be spent in hospitals.

MOM'S THANKSGIVING

Mom asks about Jiichan and Obaachan

and shows us a plate of Thanksgiving
dropped off by American church ladies.

She is thankful to have a taste of America.
She gives me and Papa a nibble
puts the plate in her room refrigerator
and says she will save a bite of pumpkin pie
to eat with Grandpa Bob and Nana
on the phone on Thanksgiving Day
California time.

Mom tells us she's tired

of the hospital milk-producing diet
even though it is tasty.

"They make the best miso soup here," she says.

Complaining
about the long hospital stay
—"doctors here are so conservative"—
she quickly adds
she is "thankful to stay with Miki."

NOVEMBER 23, 2001

BABY'S FIRST THANKSGIVING

We circle Miki
in her glass box
and list our thanks.

I am thankful Masa ignores me,
but I wish I hadn't hit him.
I don't say any of that out loud;
I'm keeping it to myself.

I am thankful Miki is a girl.
I am thankful Miki is getting stronger.
I am thankful Miki is healthy.

Mom and Papa say the same
(except the girl part).

We all agree
every day with Miki is Thanksgiving.

Papa and I have a hard time
leaving Miki
leaving Mom
but we have to go.

JIICHAN'S THANKSGIVING

Late afternoon,
lunch of
stewed vegetables
fish
miso soup
a bowl of rice
and tofu
is pushed aside on his tray table.

Papa sighs and says, "Looks good."

"Not like Mother's," Jiichan says.

Papa agrees and doesn't say
anything about eating at the ramen shop
three times a week since we've been gone.

My mouth waters
my stomach begs
Obaachan and I aren't eating many hot meals.

I hand Jiichan his rice bowl
humming a song I know he likes,
"I Look Up as I Walk."

Papa asks, "Do you know
Americans call it 'Sukiyaki'?"

"A beef dish song!"

Jiichan smiles.

I tell him, "Please get strong."

He eats for me.

WALKING TO OBAACHAN'S

Papa flags the *yaki imo* truck.
Its recording blasts encouragement to buy
but the toasty aroma is encouragement enough.

The seller bags three of his biggest roasted potatoes.
Papa hands them to me.

They warm my heart all the way back.

A HOT MEAL

Obaachan presents us
a home-cooked meal.

She dragged out the *kotatsu*
to replace the dinner table.
Our legs are cozy
draped by the blanket at the table edge and
toasted by the heater underneath the tabletop.

I am thankful for this tasty hot meal
with Papa.

Over steaming teacups, we view
a ray of sunset in the maple tree,
deepening to valentine red.

He doesn't want to leave,
but he has to go back.
Off on Friday for Labor Thanksgiving,
he has to work all weekend.

I am alone with Obaachan again.

Now there is a heater
to warm up to, but
that doesn't mean she's going to turn it on.

GIVING THANKS ON THE PHONE

Grandpa Bob and Nana on one side
of the Pacific Ocean,

me on the other side

waves of electrical pulses
bounce off a satellite
circling Earth

between us

the connection is clear.

We talk about the things
we are thankful for

warm and cozy things
we remember

driving down to San Francisco,
the coldest summer vacation ever,

flying out to New York City,
the coldest spring break ever, and

being together.

A WARM AND COZY THING

Without my complaining,

Papa sends a cloth cover
to warm up
the toilet seat.

SCHOOL ART EXHIBITION

Papa cannot come
Mom cannot come
Jiichan cannot come

I do not want Obaachan to come.

We carry our projects to the gym.

Masa is proud of his Sun painting even though
he used crayons, not paint.
His exploding Sun is yellow and green.

I heard him tell Yuta, "The inside of the Sun is green."

Our class table is crowded with projects.

Sachiko's bandaged tower and my purple heart
sit side by side.

I tell her I like her tower.

She thinks my heart is good.

NOVEMBER 29, 2001

GUITARS GENTLY WEEP

Every night
on the phone
with Papa,
I want to tell him
everything bothersome.

I talk,
but I don't say

anything worrisome.

Tonight
I hear
in Papa's voice

something sad.

His favorite Beatle died.

George Harrison passed away in California
on November twenty-ninth.

"He was a man of peace," Papa says.
"He knew how to treat people."

This would not be a good time
to tell Papa I hit Masa.

NOVEMBER 30, 2001

DECEMBER 2001

SAD AND HAPPY IN ONE DAY

Today,
America's seventh of December,
our eighth,
is a very sad anniversary—
Pearl Harbor.

Prayers are said
on all shores.

Today
sixty years later
the American president says
Japan and America
"are working side by side
in the fight against terror."

Today,
our eighth,
is a happy day—

the royal baby Aiko,
the late Emperor Hirohito's great-granddaughter,
leaves the Imperial Household Agency Hospital
in the arms of her smiling mother, Crown Princess Masako,
with Crown Prince Naruhito smiling by her side.

DECEMBER 8, 2001

ABOVE IT ALL

My thoughts are lost in space with
Grandpa Bob's NASA news:

Over six thousand small flags, and
flags from the towers,
the Pentagon
the Pennsylvania Capitol
are orbiting Earth in the Endeavor space shuttle
along with possessions of victims,
firefighters, and police officers.

A ceremony will be held
on December 11, 2001, New York time
in the International Space Station
to commemorate the loss of life on September 11.
It will be on NASA TV.
I cannot watch
without Internet access here.

I look up as I walk along
to the train station with Obaachan.

BACK TO EARTH

I stop in my tracks—

Masa!

and his mother
are standing outside a cake shop
the one with the best Christmas cake
the one with the dancing Santa
the one with the sign saying,

Please do not touch Santa.

Masa is pointing at Santa
leaning in too close
about to touch him
but doesn't.

Bashi!
His mother smacks him on the head.

Obaachan nudges me
tells me not to linger
or to watch.
She doesn't know
who this boy is.

And I don't tell her.

SITTING NEXT TO OBAACHAN

On the train
my brain
rushes—

MASA'S MOTHER hits him.
Masa's mother HITS him.
Masa's mother hits HIM.

clatters—

MASA hit me.
Masa HIT me.
Masa hit ME.

screeches—

I hit Masa.
I HIT Masa.
I hit MASA.

My stomach sinks with motion.
My heart is sicker.
My face is an open book.

I feel
a woman
Obaachan's age

looking at me
looking at
Obaachan
looking
at us
watching
seeing
feeling
sensing
knowing
I am about to leave
she slips something
into my hand.

ON THE PLATFORM

I look down into the face
of a small origami doll
smiling up at me

her arms open wide
a heart glued to her sash.

She is mostly heart.

Covered in plastic
a slit of paper stuck on the outside
says

May Peace Prevail on Earth

in English.

Obaachan bends over the doll,
looks me in the eyes,
asks,

"What is the meaning?"

The *meaning*.
I don't know "prevail."

I look at Obaachan
in her eyes

for the first time
I see black spokes around her pupils.

Like mine.

I am like Obaachan.

But worse.
She doesn't hit.
I do.

THE MEANING

I look down
and
see the big heart.

Without translation,
without hesitation,
without intimidation,
I tell Obaachan, "Put peace in your heart."

She looks like someone has seen her
sweeping with the wrong broom.

She shrinks,
recoils,
strikes out
toward the exit.

This stranger has seen into our hearts.

OBAACHAN'S UNFOLDING LOVE

Between Earth and Sun
Moon is passing
in an annular solar eclipse
we cannot see from Japan.

I am watching
looking for
and seeing
cosmic changes
in this house.

DECEMBER 14, 2001

WITHOUT FUSSING

Obaachan and I prepare for Mom and Miki
to leave the hospital.

We dust,
vacuum,
and pull out a space heater
for Great-Grandfather's room.

Obaachan doesn't notice the messy-looking ceiling.
She doesn't fuss once all day.

That's cosmic.

AND A TOASTY MOMENT

Obaachan doesn't notice
the hole at the big toe
of my sock
before I slide my legs
under the heater table.

Drinking tea alone
together
for the first time

ever

she notices
I fold back the peel of a *mikan,*
into one star-shaped piece
and use it as a plate
for the juicy orange wedges I pull apart.

She tells me
for the first time in my life,
"You know manners."

I tuck the sock hole
between my toes

and smile.

RED RICE

Obaachan places one thousand yen in my hand
scoots me out of the house
tells me where to go
to buy *sekihan* for Mom and Miki's
"homecoming."

Mom would prefer Western cake,
Obaachan knows that, but
I know red rice is for celebrations.

I go all the way to Mr. Iida's shop
to give him our business.
I pass
Mr. Tanaka's cake shop.
Western cakes. New York cheesecake,
Mom's favorite
three hundred yen a slice.

I open Iida's shop door
shouting,
"Excuse me!"

He clamors downstairs
slips into slippers
stands behind the counter
wiping his mouth.

I smell salty soy rice crackers on his face.
I have interrupted his teatime.

"Red rice," I say.

He says, "Congratulations."

PRESENTATION

Mom's bags are packed
waiting for Papa

I am there
with Obaachan when the nurse
presents Mom with a small wooden box.

I ask if I can open it.
Mom looks at Obaachan,
says yes.

They smile.

Inside
on clipped cotton
is the piece of umbilical cord
that dried and fell
from Miki's belly button—

a souvenir of the cord
binding mother and baby.

Little Sister is entering the world.
Mom is returning

with softer eyes.

HOME

Papa arrives with a small bag of his own
for only one night with us.
We settle in.

Later, cozy with us all together
in Great-Grandfather's room,
he says,

"I miss home."

I stand up, pull the light cord, and tell them to look up.

kira, kira
a view of
fifty sparkling stars.

We have a good laugh together.

SLEEPING SISTER

After school
I can't wait to be with Miki.

I read to her,
practice the pianika
and do my homework next to her
and the heater,

but she sleeps all the time
I am with her.

She looks nothing like me.
She's smaller than I ever was
which means she will probably always be small.
Not like me at all.

The first time
she opens her eyes
and looks at me
I see she has eyes

just like Papa's
just like Obaachan's
just like mine.

NO CHRISTMAS DECORATIONS

With end-of-the-year obligations
Papa has no time

to dig decorations out
at home.
We won't see him until
Christmas.

He tells me to ask Obaachan
to bring out their Christmas tree,
the one Jiichan bought when Papa was a boy.

Mom tells her not to bother.
Obaachan says the tree has been gone for decades.

No Christmas tree?

I suggest cutting a branch from the garden.

And making paper decorations.

Mom tells me in English, "We can do without."

Mom is a little like Obaachan.
She doesn't want what she doesn't want.

A PACKAGE IN THE MAIL

Addressed from Nana and Grandpa Bob,
it's wrapped in brown paper
on the outside
and
underneath
in red paper
with a note
saying,
Don't wait till Christmas!

Opened wide, it smells
like America
like Nana's laundry room
where her washer and dryer share a room of their own,
a room where she keeps boxes for sending us things.

This box is filled with smaller packages for us all.

A note on Mom's (the biggest) says, "A wish fulfilled."

The Easy-Bake Oven
she always wanted,
but never got until now

guarantees she'll get a Western cake.

For Papa
a package that feels like socks.

For Obaachan and Jiichan
a jar of grape jelly.
They tried mine once and liked it.
Obaachan accepted it with a smile.

For me
a video in English.
Pokémon
(Pocket Monsters
have an American name.)

For Miki
a bear sleeping on a crescent moon.
For "Baby's First Christmas" tree.

A PACKAGE IN THE ENTRY HALL

Wrapped in department-store paper,
a narrow box greets me after school.
Obaachan says it is for us.
Mom and Miki and me.
An early present. From her.
We open it together in the TV room.

A Pocket Monsters Christmas tree.

Mom gasps
busies herself
with baby things.

I tell Obaachan thank you.

I know
Mom doesn't like the tree.
She doesn't like cartoon Christmas decorations.
She doesn't say anything
until Obaachan leaves the room,

"She never buys anything and she buys *this*."

I can't believe Mom's complaining
about a Christmas tree

about a gift.

TRAIN ANGEL

I look at my little sister
sleeping
my little sister
listening
my little sister

learning.

I show and tell Mom about the origami doll.

I tell her
what Masa did to me
what I did to Masa
and what I told Obaachan
the meaning is.

I tell her I am trying to put peace in my heart.

I tell her I think Obaachan is trying too.

Mom takes the doll
from my hands,
places it on the tree,
and says,
"You're right."

Later I hear her
thanking Obaachan for the tree.

After tasting an Easy-Bake Oven cake,
Obaachan smiles
and does not comment.

These, I believe, are Christmas miracles.

A CHANGE OF HEART

Mom tells me we must talk
to the teacher, Masa's mother, and Masa
after the holidays,
saying the same thing Obaachan said,
"Even an accident requires an apology."

I hit Masa.
It was no accident.

I tell Mom I will apologize
first
before Christmas.

A DOLL FOR MASA

At Papa's desk,
I dig through origami paper.

Stripes, Masa wears stripes.

Folding
cutting
pasting
I make a faceless boy doll.

I place him beside the girl doll.
She smiles up at me.
Her eyes are tiny dots.
Her smile, just a line.

Whoever drew this face knew
how to make a sweet face
how to give a sweet smile.

Eyes not too small,
not too close together.

A smile not too big,
not too curved.

Dots and lines.
It's not easy.

Wish I had my NASA pen.

I know the feel of it in my hand.

I need it

to draw this face.

DOLL FACE

I choose a brush
one with the finest tip
from the set
Papa used to address wedding invitations.

I dribble water
poto poto

from a porcelain water pot
onto Great-Grandfather's inkstone.

su su su su
back and forth
round and round
I rub an ink stick,
its name
"The Friend of Brush,"
on the stone.

I rub it into the puddle
with a soft touch.

Too much force will ruin the ink.

Stick on stone
stick and stone
meet.

Ink strengthens
water.
I lead it to the well,
the sea of the stone.

Brush meets ink
I introduce the paper.
The boy's eyes stare up at me.
Without the smile I cannot tell the feeling.

After a thousand smiles
on practice paper,
I take a breath
and draw one line
on the boy's face.

Sweet.

CHANGING HEARTS

Drawing a heart isn't easy either.

I waste paper
drawing and cutting
writing and deciding
on the message.

The yellow-green paper heart I make
is as big as the boy,
but I can't decide on a message
short enough to fit inside.

The writing becomes too tiny
too hard to read.

Masa will have to read it quickly
before he tosses it
back at me.

MAKING PEACE WITH OBAACHAN

Fifth graders know the kanji
heiwa,
peace among nations,
peace among people.

We have not studied how to write
the kanji for peace in the heart, *heion*.

I ask Obaachan to teach me.
Stroke by stroke, I know
I will have to use
the one I know
Masa can read.

I tell her that one English word
is used to find
peace among nations
peace among people
peace in the heart.

Obaachan says Masa will understand my meaning.

I write the kanji for heiwa.

"Peace among people"
fills his heart.

MAKING PEACE WITH MASA

I find him at the shoe shelves after school.

He's knocking
the toes of his shoes onto the floor
ready and set
to run out the door.
I jump in front of him and reach out
with the doll.

"I'm sorry," I say.

He clenches his hand
swings his arm

reaches out

takes the doll,
takes one look at it,
and takes off
running.

BEAUTIFUL DAY

I almost run
to Obaachan
to Mom
to Miki

to tell them
there is hope.

They meet me with good news.

Jiichan will leave the hospital soon!

ON THE NEWS

At a gathering at the Uwajima Fisheries High School

one hundred and twenty boxes
of personal items
recovered from victims,
students, teachers, crew members of the *Ehime Maru*
are given to their families;

to the principal
the school flag from the ship

to the captain
a bell from the steering room.

Heartbroken,

we all pledge to limit
Jiichan's TV viewing
when he comes back.

DECEMBER 20, 2001

LOOKING UP

After school
we all run out
lift our faces
to snowflakes

anticipating
weekend fun.

Snowflakes drift
by the window, while
Mom dries my hair.

Obaachan fusses
as she leaves, saying
Jiichan's return
will be difficult.

For the first time in my life
I am glad it stops snowing.

DECEMBER 21, 2001

JIICHAN'S HOMECOMING

He and Obaachan arrive by taxi.

He is
refreshed
like
from a long vacation,

a "soul vacation."

His eyes are smiling above the mask
he wears for Miki
"just in case."

Obaachan bought *yuzu*
to float in the bath
to warm the body
to calm the mind
and *kabocha*
to eat at dinner.

Funny to think
citrus fruit is bobbing in bathtubs
and Japanese pumpkin is boiling in pots
all over Japan
on this night of the winter solstice.

DECEMBER 21, 2001

DEFENSE OF JIICHAN

Mom told me
Papa told her

doctors told Obaachan
to create a less stressful home
for Jiichan's heart.

We let him watch a comedy
while waiting for the bath to fill.

He is first in line,
sniffs the yuzu,
"Nice, eh?"
and heads for the bath
to soak with them.

We have timed his bath at the news.

Planes and boats chase
a North Korean boat
and exchange gunfire
off the shore of Japan.

Obaachan switches off the TV
before Jiichan comes out.

Shriveled pink
like a plum

he falls asleep at the table
and snores.

Nobody disturbs him.

DECEMBER 21, 2001

UNDER WINTER TREES

The sunniest time of year in the garden
Jiichan, in his quilted house jacket,
sits and enjoys

mejiro,
the green-feathered
acrobat of the treetops.

He's not supposed to climb
to water the bonsai,
but he wants to

so I let him.

The pail is not so heavy;
not much water is needed now.

I am the lookout for Obaachan, but
I think he can get away with it—
nobody wants to bring him down.

He can do anything he wants.
Except smoke.
And watch the news.

HOLIDAY PREPARATION

Teacher explains
our holiday assignments,
hands us
worksheets of math,
schedules of reading assignments,
and a tight white paper roll
of five sheets
to practice our *kakizome*
at home.

Then, with her back to us,
she leads us

stroke by stroke

we trace the air
together
before our brushes
touch paper.

Stones ready
with bottled ink
we brush

a message
to practice
for our first calligraphy writing of the new year.

HAPPY BIRTHDAY TO THE EMPEROR

Two days off for Papa and me:
Sunday
and Christmas Eve!

We decided no presents from each other
this year. But I have secret plans for later.

Jiichan and Obaachan enjoy toast and their grape jelly
from Grandpa Bob and Nana.

Mom bakes another Easy Bake cake
(and does not have to share).

Papa relaxes in his cozy socks.

(With him) I watch Miki
not Pokémon.

Grandpa Bob and Nana call to say
NASA will track Santa!

Merry Christmas to all!

SO THIS IS CHRISTMAS

Santa found me
at Obaachan's!
A present sits and will wait
for me under the Pocket Monster tree.
Papa leaves for work before
I get up
for just another school day,
the last one until January eighth

except today we sing "Silent Night"
and "Rudolph the Red-nosed Reindeer"
and
Teacher hands out report cards.
Some students look;
others slide them into their book bags.

Teacher hands me an official paper
(not my official card)
with grades,

all okay but not great.
All my flower heads full and plucked
translated into lower numbers
than my usual high grades.

I am not going to let that ruin my Christmas.

PRESENT RETURNED

Saying no to invitations
to play on the playground,
I start alone
slower than I want to.

Loaded down
with art projects and school bags,
I am followed
by the sun
peeping through the clouds.

I see something
twinkling
like a fallen star.

My NASA pen!

Stuck in the dirt next to the sidewalk
so I would find it

my blue-sky wish
still inside.

Best Christmas ever!

OPENING

Santa brought me a music player
with headphones.
Papa will help me
pick out some music
when he comes for the New Year's holiday.

We said no presents but
Obaachan bought a small Christmas cake
yellow sponge
whipped-cream frosting
strawberries between
knob flowers
with optional birthday candles

not Mom's favorite
but she's not complaining.

I gave the Sun painting to
Mom and Papa (when he comes).

I bought Obaachan a bottle of vinegar.
I have heard her say, "Useful presents are best."

I gave Jiichan the purple heart.

I plan to give Miki
her first look at the night sky.

PRESENT RECEIVED

Grandpa Bob and Nana
called to say thank you to everyone
for the handkerchiefs.

Brought back memories for them;
they used to carry handkerchiefs in the old days.

"Supermoon on the twenty-eighth," Grandpa Bob tells me.

I have to wait
to give Miki her present.

But I hope her first moon will be SUPER.

ENDING AND BEGINNING

Christmas is put away
the day after

New Year's decorations go up
along the way
to the station
outside shops

at gates

branches of pine
welcome good fortune.

The peace doll sits on top of
postal cards stacked
ready for addressing
New Year's wishing.

I have my NASA pen!

OLD ROUTINE WITH CHANGES

I know the routine of this time of year
with Obaachan and Jiichan

cleaning from rafters to tatami
from soles to pedals
from garden stones to gate.

This year Jiichan will rest.
This year Obaachan lets Mom
and me
help prepare food
to last the first three days of the new year.

Papa arrives in a taxi
with our electric carpet rolled and
hanging out the window.

He vacuums the tatami in Great-Grandfather's room,
rolls out the carpet, and plugs it in.
Our futons will be warmer at night.

Obaachan places my favorite New Year's food,
candied chestnuts with sweet potatoes,
along with other not-so-favorite food (dried sardines)
in lacquer boxes decorated with golden
plum blossom, bamboo, and pine,
the luckiest combination.

Looks like
sounds like
feels like
a happy home.

NEW YEAR'S EVE 2001

Three days of
watching TV (screened for Jiichan)
feasting
receiving greeting cards

begins with
the *Red and White Song Battle* on TV,
noodles at midnight,
the shrine bell gong on TV,
money envelopes (small change this year),
and

the first dream of the new year.

A dream hopefully of
an eggplant, a hawk, or Mount Fuji.

All three is the luckiest dream.

Jiichan and I are lucky already;
our favorite singers, the white team,
won the song battle.

BROKEN HEARTS

TV and the newspaper
show us
the fallen towers
the hollow field
the gaping war department—

the rubble

the scars

on millions of hearts.

It's difficult to screen everything for Jiichan
until his heart is strong again.

LOOKING BACK

I show Mom and Papa the grade paper.
and they congratulate me on Teacher's comments:
Ema worked hard
and improved.

After hearing the Masa story
Papa says he agrees with Mom,
we must talk to Teacher,
Masa, and his mother
after the holiday
and says,

"Bullies need to know they are seen."

I agree.

But I am not looking forward to it.

AND AHEAD

The new year is already here
when Nana calls with spring visit plans.

I tell Grandpa Bob I don't remember
my new year's first dream.

He tells me
no matter what
New Year's is a time to think about
possibilities,
beginning again,
or starting something new.

"Think with 'future hope' in mind," he says.

I can hear him smiling

and later, feasting,
Jiichan raises a slice of lotus root to his eye
squints through one of the holes
and says,
"I see a better year ahead."

He does this every new year, but this year
he is looking at Miki sleeping on a cushion.

TRADITIONAL SECOND-DAY TASK

Papa watches over me
while I prepare
paper
brush
inkstone
ink stick, and
water pot

poto poto
su su su
against the stone
I rub stick into water into ink.

With the school practice paper as a guide
stroke by stroke

BRIGHT HEART
appears on the paper.

I hang it to dry
next to a scroll of painted sparrows.

The first day back at school,
we will hang this message
in the hallway
to remind us
to polish our hearts
with kindness toward one another.

BRIGHTER HEARTS

I put the peace doll
on top of the TV
to remind us

a new year
a new beginning
a new chance has come

to try better
to do better
to be better.

While listening to the story of the doll,
Jiichan's eyes sparkle.

JANUARY 2, 2002

ACKNOWLEDGMENTS

Gratitude to Daddy, Carol Baker, Mrs. Eldridge and Mr. Richard Jenkins, Nancy Kirwan Rinehart, and Jan Oppie for early writing encouragement; SCBWI-Japan, Kent Brown and The Highlights Foundation, Virginia Euwer Wolff, Sonya Sones, and Linda Oatman High for guidance; the Highlights Novel in Verse Sisterhood, especially Debra Rook, Carol Coven Grannick, Liz Heywood, Kathy Mirkin, and Sandra Armistead Havriluk for encouragement and guidance; Yoko Yoshizawa, Naomi Kojima, Gerri Sorrells, Chiyo Hayashi, and the Chikamatsu family for clarity.

Thank you Holly McGhee for giving this story a chance, nuturing it, and finding it a home. Thank you, Courtney Stevenson. And to Caitlyn Dlouhy, who gave this story a place in the world along with Sonia Chaghatzbanian, Clare McGlade, and Elizabeth Blake-Linn at Caitlyn Dlouhy Books, Atheneum, my deepest gratitude and admiration.